THE EARL TAKES A WIFE

A de Courtenay Novella

SHERRY EWING

Copyright © 2019 by Sherry Ewing

All rights reserved.

No part of this book may be reproduced in any form or by any electronic or mechanical means, including information storage and retrieval systems, without written permission from the author, except for the use of brief quotations in a book review.s

Kingsburg Pres
P.O. Box 475146
San Francisco, CA 94147
www.kingsburgpress.com

The Earl Takes A Wife is a work of fiction. Names, characters, places, and incidents are a product of the author's imagination. Locales and public names are sometimes used for atmospheric purposes. Any resemblance to actual people, living or dead, or to businesses, companies, events, institutions, or locales is completely coincidental.

Other characters mentioned in this story belonging to the Bluestocking Belles remain with their author. I thank them for allowing me to continue to use them in *The Earl Takes A Wife*.

Front Cover Design:
www.SelfPubBookCovers.com/3rustedspoons
Back Cover Design: by Sherry Ewing

The Earl Takes A Wife/Sherry Ewing -- 1st ed.
ISBN eBook: 978-1-946177-94-0
ISBN Print: 978-1-946177-91-9
Library of Congress Control Number: 2019915147

OTHER BOOKS BY SHERRY EWING

Medieval & Time Travel Series

*To Love A Scottish Laird: De Wolfe Pack
Connected World*

If My Heart Could See You: The MacLaren's

For All of Ever: The Knights of Berwyck,

A Quest Through Time (Book One)

Only For You: The Knights of Berwyck,

A Quest Through Time (Book Two)

Hearts Across Time: The Knights of Berwyck,

A Quest Through Time (Books One & Two)

A special box set of For All of Ever & Only For You

A Knight To Call My Own: The MacLaren's

To Follow My Heart: The Knights of Berwyck,

A Quest Through Time (Book Three)

The Piper's Lady within *Never Too Late*: A Bluestocking
Belles Collection 2017

Love Will Find You: The Knights of Berwyck,

A Quest Through Time (Book Four), Coming Soon

One Last Kiss: The Knights of Berwyck,

A Quest Through Time (Book Five)

Regency's

A Kiss for Charity*: A de Courtenay Novella (Book One)*

The Earl Takes A Wife*: A de Courtenay Novella (Book Two)*

Nothing But Time, *A Family of Worth: Book One*

One Moment In Time*: A Family of Worth, Book Two*

Under the Mistletoe

Join Sherry's newsletter at http://bit.ly/2vGrqQM

www.SherryEwing.com

THE EARL TAKES A WIFE

For My Readers

No matter if I write medieval, time travel, or Regency era stories, I thank each and every one of you for your support throughout the years. You are the reason I continue to write. Without you, I'd still be sitting in my writing cave wondering if my stories would ever be good enough to self-publish. From your reviews and friendship, I think you've proven to me that they are.

Thank you. This one's for you!

PROLOGUE

Hollystone Hall
January, 1813

Lord Adrian de Courtenay hurried through the many corridors of Hollystone Hall until he at last found the library. His gaze swept around the room until he saw his book where he had left it on one of the side tables next to an overstuffed chair. As he crossed the room, he heard a soft click behind him and turned at the noise.

He was surprised to see Lady Celia Lacey leaning up against the wood. She was a pretty little bird, and he had considered pursuing her perhaps once she was a little older. The girl was barely out of the schoolroom after all, no more than ten and six years... seven at the most. His taste had never been for young virgins, but

1

something pulled at his heartstrings when she continued to follow him around during the house party. Her blonde hair bounced invitingly whenever she rushed to catch up to him on many an occasion, but her lovesick blue eyes reminded Adrian she was too young and innocent to flirt with.

Even if he had considered giving into the temptation she represented, the situation had changed once he became aware his sister, Grace, and Lady Celia's uncle, Lord Nicholas, had developed an affection for one another. If Gracie and Lord Nicholas were to wed, Celia would be family. Getting involved with her was highly ill advised.

Lady Celia's eyes widened once they leveled upon him from across the room. He picked up the book, holding it close to his chest. As he approached, a smile lit her face. What was his little sparrow up to? More importantly... what was she doing here without her chaperone?

"Are you leaving?" she blurted out when he drew near. Her tone verged on panic. Her hand rose to her neck as if to free a breath suddenly caught in her throat.

God, but she was going to be a beauty once she left the girl behind and became a woman full grown. A part of him was flattered, knowing he was the cause of her current state of breathlessness. He envied the man who would one day claim her as his wife. He was going to be one lucky man.

"Yes. My sisters, Grace and Miranda, and I were walking to our carriage when I remembered this," he said, giving the book he held a wave in the air. "And you? Are you departing today, as well?"

"Tomorrow. My oldest sister, Elinor, is tidying up several details from the charity ball."

"I suspect, before long, we shall all be family, if Grace and your uncle have anything to say on the matter." Adrian assumed there would be a wedding celebration in the near future.

"Do you think so?" she whispered, her eyes bright with excitement. "We would see each other often if they were to marry."

Adrian cleared his throat, stepping several paces backwards to distance himself. She, in turn, advanced. "Yes, well... I suppose such may be the case. Time will tell."

"Time... yes... time is all we need. Will you wait for me Lord de Courtenay... Adrian?"

"W-wait for you?" he stammered. "Where the devil is your chaperon?" Good Lord, what had he gotten himself into? This situation had gotten out of hand faster than he ever expected. He went around her to open the door, but the key was missing. Turning back, she waved what he needed.

"Looking for this?" she laughed.

The little scamp! "Lady Celia," Adrian began, holding his palm upward. "The key, if you please."

She laughed. "Oh, very well," she replied, handing the shiny brass object over; it was still warm from her touch. "You do not have to be so formal. As you said, we might be related one day."

Adrian turned the key in the lock and opened the door. "All the more reason to adhere to the rules of Society. You are the daughter of a duke and should not be alone with a single male, especially me."

A giggle of girlish delight burst from her lips. "I am certain I am perfectly safe in your company, Adrian," she said, dropping all formality between them.

He watched when her perfect little mouth lifted up into an enchanting smile. This young woman needed to be kissed and often. "Do you think so?" he asked, stepping closer, wishing to teach her a lesson. Her eyes widened. Was this just a game to her? Was she as flirtatious as his younger sister Miranda had become? No... something sincere shone in her face. The girl had no hidden agendas... or did she?

"W-why, y-yes... of c-course, I am," she stuttered, suddenly appearing unsure of herself as her confidence in their situation tipped and not in her favor.

He lifted her chin with one finger to stare into her sparkling blue eyes. If she was expecting to be kissed, she would be sadly mistaken. He did not dally with troublesome virgins. He did not. He had a mistress who could see to his needs. Still... he leaned forward, and a soft floral scent swirled around his senses.

"You have a lot to learn about men, little one,"

Adrian whispered into her ear and felt her shiver. He should not be teasing her so, but he could not seem to help himself. "Trust me when I tell you to set your cap for someone else. You are far too young for me."

Her hand went to his arm as though to hold on for support. "You sound as though you are ancient, my lord. I am certainly old enough to become your wife."

"Wife?" he exclaimed, stepping back as though she had the plague. Heaven forbid! She *was* set on a marriage between them. "Whatever makes you think I am ready to take a wife?"

Her brows met as she pondered. "Certainly you must be considering marriage to someone, my lord. Why not let that lady be me?"

Damn, she was a brave one and far more outspoken than he thought for someone of her tender years. Before he could answer her outrageous bid to become his wife, they heard her name being called from down the hallway.

Once more taking hold of his arm, she pulled him forward before lifting herself up on the tips of her toes to place a quick kiss upon his cheek. "Please wait for me, Adrian..." she whispered in a soft plea against his ear. Without waiting for his answer, she picked up the hem of her dress and ran from the room.

Adrian stood there, stunned. Where had his little sparrow found the nerve to leave him with her kiss? He lifted his hand to his cheek, still feeling the warmth of her breath on his face. He needed a few minutes to compose himself before he could join his sisters in their carriage. Taking a deep breath, he shut the library door and left Hollystone Hall. Once in London, he turned to his usual gentlemanly pursuits and tried to forget the lovely Lady Celia. She would haunt his dreams for many months to come...

CHAPTER 1

London
Summer, 1813

L ady Celia Lacey's grip upon her crystal champagne flute was tight enough that she was in danger of snapping the stem. Her parents' ballroom was filled to capacity in celebration of the wedding of her Uncle Nicholas and Lady Grace de Courtenay. Celia had not seen her beloved uncle so happy in a long while. After the horrible accident that took his first wife, Celia was glad he had found love again. It gave her hope... almost.

She watched the couple dancing to the lively tune of a quadrille, trying to ignore the pain in her heart as she saw *him* with another woman on his arm. Adrian... *so much for him waiting for her*. He must have thought her the silliest girl in all of England when she had whispered her heartfelt desires while at Hollystone. Since then, Adrian seemed to go out of his way to have one woman after another upon his arm whenever he and Celia were thrown together.

"They make a striking pair, do they not?"

They did indeed, much to her annoyance, and she almost sighed aloud when a lock of his brown hair fell rakishly across his brow. The lady he escorted tonight laughed at something he said when they came together in the dance, causing the green-eyed monster of jealousy to rear its ugly head.

"Lady Celia?"

Celia turned to see Adrian's sister Miranda at her side. "My apologies, Miss de Courtenay. You were saying?"

Miranda gave a gentle laugh. "I must insist you call me by my first name. We are now family, after all."

Celia nodded. "Of course. You must call me Celia."

Miranda looped her arm through Celia's. "I was saying they make a striking pair," she repeated.

Celia gave a heavy sigh. "I daresay they do," she replied, trying to keep a polite smile upon her face. Even to her own ears, her tone sounded frightfully less than encouraging. She took a large sip of her champagne.

"I thought you would be happy for my sister and your uncle." A frown crossed Miranda's brow. "Although I *am* feeling a bit left out not having a title of my own."

"I beg your pardon?" Celia asked, before handing

her glass to a passing servant and reaching for another flute.

Miranda discreetly pointed with her glass toward the newly-wedded couple. "Are you not pleased they are now wed?"

Celia's faced flushed with heat as she realized her mistake. "Oh! Yes, I am very pleased for them. My cousin has told me nothing but good things about Lady Grace, who has taken Blanche under her wing as if she always belonged there."

"Then whatever has you so flustered? Should I accompany you to the balcony for some fresh air?" Miranda inquired in concern.

Celia once more searched out the face that had haunted her every moment since she first laid eyes upon him months ago at Hollystone Hall. Was it just a coincidence when their eyes met from across the room? Coincidence that he missed a step while he attempted to keep his eyes upon her as the dance continued?

"Oh goodness! You are in love with my brother!" Miranda exclaimed.

Bother. The young woman had figured out just whom Celia had been staring at.

"I said no such thing, Miss de Courtenay," Celia hissed, reverting back to a formal address in an attempt to calm the girl, who appeared ecstatic about the situation.

"You did not have to, Celia. I can see for myself you hold an affection for him. But I must warn you, his taste in women has never been for someone of your tender years. I would hate to see you hurt."

"Adrian would never hurt me," she rebutted in his defense.

"*Adrian*, is it?" Miranda said with a smirk of satisfaction. "Does he know you care for him?"

"I– I asked him to wait for me when he left Hollystone Hall. I can see for myself my gesture meant little to him given he brought a lady to the wedding reception." Celia snapped open her fan and waved it before her flushed face. She prayed it concealed her crestfallen features, though clearly the lady standing next to her had seen enough.

"Adrian can be a brute when it comes to matters of the heart. Why, he berated me for months about that little incident that caught me... unaware of what was truly going on around me." Miranda's cheeks flushed as she apparently relived the memory of her brother's scolding, or perhaps, of her own behavior at the masquerade ball at Hollystone Hall.

"Little?" Celia asked, her brows rose at the audacity of the woman next to her. "If I may be blunt, Miranda, you were lucky to come away with your reputation intact. Even I know the Marquis of Aldridge is not someone to trifle with, let alone to expect a proposal of marriage from."

Miranda had the decency to appear contrite. "Yes... well... I suppose you have that correct. Still... I never thought I would hear the end of Adrian's babbling about finding me a proper husband. I have in no uncertain terms told him I will wed when the right gentleman with a title crosses my path. I will settle for nothing less."

Celia regarded the woman, who was several years older than her. "Love tends to find you when you least expect it. What if the perfect gentleman happens by, and he does not have a title but is perfectly respectable in every other way?"

"A gentleman with a *title*," Miranda repeated, "and nothing less. I refuse to be the only one in my family without one." Her lips snapped shut as though she had also closed her mind to any other possibilities.

"I hope you find him, then, Miranda," Celia said. "Everyone deserves to find someone to love and titles tend to get in the way of finding true happiness."

"Including you?" Miranda asked as she took Celia's arm.

"Yes. I want nothing more than for the man I marry to love me for me and not because of the riches that will come to him because I am a duke's daughter. I suppose if he has a title of his own, that will be one less obstacle to believing his true intentions."

"A man like my brother?" Miranda asked with a laugh.

Celia blushed at the thought of being Adrian's wife. Such an outcome had been at the forefront of her mind since she met the man. If only he would think of her as a grown woman instead of a child. "He would make a most suitable husband. Even my parents would approve."

Miranda burst into laughter, then clamped her lips shut and composed herself. "My apologies, Celia. I just had this image of my older brother falling for a young lady of your inexperienced years. Why, he acts as though he knows *everything* about women, which is hardly the case. For him to fall for you would be completely out of character for him, but I swear it would be most enjoyable to watch his downfall. I might even have my revenge after all he said to me about my behavior at Hollystone."

Celia shook her head. "I am not certain if I should be laughing with you or upset you have somehow insulted me," she declared, frowning. A sudden thought struck her. "Perhaps you could teach me to be more... flirtatious, so I might capture your brother's attention?"

A sound erupted from Miranda that was half laugh, half snort. She recovered herself quickly. "I am not sure that is a good idea. Adrian would never approve..." she replied, but Celia did not miss the sudden sparkle that lit Miranda's eyes.

"Does it matter if he approves or not?" Celia asked, unsure where such a question came from.

Miranda gave Celia a quick hug. "I think you and I are going to become the best of friends."

Celia smiled until her eyes once more found Adrian's across the crowded room. The dance had ended, and he had just handed his escort a glass of wine. He scowled in

Celia's direction, but for the life of her, she could not think what she had done to make such a frown appear upon his handsome face.

She had no more time to consider the matter, for he excused himself from the lady at his side and began striding in her direction. God help her to remember to say something witty in order to keep his attention. Or to breathe... yes... she constantly needed to remember to breathe whenever Adrian de Courtenay was near.

CHAPTER 2

Adrian marched across the crowded room with only one purpose in mind; to get Miranda away from Lady Celia. Nothing good could come from his sister's association with such an innocent; Adrian could only wonder what scheme Miranda was now concocting. He did not trust his sister. Not. One. Bit!

As he drew closer, some of his immediate anger left him. The young lady who had been at the forefront of his mind these many months despite his best efforts to forget her appeared lovely in a pale blue muslin gown with a rose-colored sash. White gloves reached to her elbows and a fan dangled from one wrist. A string of pearls was draped around her swanlike neck and matching earrings dangled elegantly from her ears. *She should be wearing jewels...* sapphires, perhaps... glittering gems only outshone by the color of her sparkling eyes. If she were his, he would spend a small fortune on jewelry, if it would but make her happy. *Good God! Where had that thought come from?*

He frowned as Miranda feverishly whispered in Celia's ear, and the young woman nodded her head as though in agreement. He hastened his step to reach the pair.

"Lady Celia," he said, bowing before he slid a glance toward his sister. "Miranda…"

"Adrian!" Miranda declared, overly loud. "Lady Celia and I were just discussing what a handsome pair Gracie and Lord Nicholas make. Would you not agree?"

He watched Celia's face flush a becoming shade of red, telling him that was not all they had been talking about. "Yes. I have never seen a happier couple," he remarked dryly. "Miranda—"

"And the music is utterly divine, is this not so, Lady Celia?" Miranda rushed on.

"Only the best musicians have been hired for my uncle and his new wife," Celia replied, her eyes twinkling in delight as she watched him.

Miranda latched onto his arm. "And can you believe this, dear brother…" She leaned forward so only the three of them could hear her words. "No one, and I repeat, no one, has even once asked Lady Celia to dance. You must change this, Adrian, at once. Go dance with her," Miranda urged, taking Celia's hand and placing it upon his arm. "Off you go now. I believe the next dance is a waltz!"

Adrian cleared his throat, feeling completely manipulated by the pair, although Celia had the decency to appear shocked. "Shall we, my lady?" he asked, feeling he had no other option if he were to not cause a scene at his sister's wedding.

Celia nodded "It would be an honor, my lord."

As if he had ordered the music to start at his command, he swung Celia into his arms and began the pattern of the waltz. A truly scandalous dance, if ever there was one, but Gracie could have whatever dance she wished, since this was a private affair. He forgot all about his sisters while he held Celia close within his arms. She was an exceptional dancer: light upon her feet, matching his steps and following where he led her upon the floor.

"Was my sister behaving herself?" he asked, suddenly feeling the need for a conversation between them. She missed a step, and he tightened his hand upon her waist to steady her.

"Y-yes, of c-course, Lord de Courtenay," Celia stammered. She kept her eyes upon his cravat as though inspecting it for some flaw, not that his valet would let him leave the house without being impeccably attired.

He chuckled. "*Lord de Courtenay?*" he murmured. Her eyes rose to his, and he noticed a bit of expectation hidden in their depths before she looked away. "What happened to you calling me 'Adrian'?"

She gave a light laugh that did not seem to suit her. "Oh, that silly notion... Why, I am surprised you remember such a trivial little thing from a mere girl."

"I never said calling each other by our first names was trivial, Celia," he said, wondering what was going on. She did not seem the same young woman whom he had met just months ago.

"Actually, I was thinking about the part of our conversation where I asked you to wait for me or for you to even consider me as your wife," she laughed again, but even he could tell the sound was forced. "Whatever was I thinking?"

"I found it quite refreshing," he said with a chuckle, "and amusing at the same time. It is not every day a man gets a possible marriage proposal from a lady."

Her lip quivered before she composed herself. "You must forgive me for my foolishness, my lord," she said so quietly Adrian almost missed hearing her words. "I promise I will not act in such a childish manner toward you again. I am certain you found the whole conversation distasteful."

"Celia, I hardly found our discussion distasteful." This was not the young vibrant woman he remembered this past winter. What in the hell had Celia and Miranda been talking about?

"Have no fear, Lord de Courtenay. I understand your need to take to wife someone far more sophisticated than I. I promise I will not do anything so foolish as embarrass you again by throwing myself at you."

"You are completely misunderstanding the situation," he roared out before he snapped his lips shut.

"Am I? Well, no matter. You have a very lovely lady

waiting for you. She appears impatient that you return to her side if craning her neck in our direction to keep an eye on you is any indication of her own agenda," Celia said offhandedly, but he would be a fool if he did not notice the glimpse of hurt shimmering in her blue eyes.

"The lady and I are barely acquainted," Adrian replied. No need to tell this innocent that the lady's appeal was her lack of the same quality, but that he had begun to regret bringing her here. Lady Sarah showed far too much interest in marriage for his liking, and he did not trust her not to try to trap him, as other women had attempted in the past.

Celia gave him a sad sort of smile. "And yet you still brought her to something as important as your sister's wedding."

The music suddenly ended to Adrian's annoyance, and he had no other option than to return the lady to Miranda's side. He was just about to ask if Celia might care for another turn about the dance floor when another stepped up to claim her.

The man bowed before her. "Lady Celia, I believe this dance is mine," he said, holding out his hand.

Celia curtseyed before placing her hand in the gentleman's as he led her to the dance floor.

Adrian's fists clenched at his side. Jealous? Of another man dancing with Celia? Why? He had no claim to her. Yet there was something in the pit of his stomach that told him in no uncertain terms that he did not care for the matter at all!

"Who the devil is that, anyway?" he snapped.

Miranda turned her gaze to the dancers swirling around the floor. "Who, Adrian?" she asked sweetly.

"You damn well know to whom I am referring," he growled out.

"Oh! Do you mean the utterly handsome Marquis of Wyndham?"

"Why am I not surprised that you know him?" Adrian muttered, while watching the couple. Where Celia was light, Wyndham was dark: his midnight black hair contrasting with Celia's blonde locks, which were arranged in a pleasing coiffure.

"We have only just been introduced this evening. I am surprised you have not heard of him but then you *have* been a bit preoccupied with your latest lady who has been holding your attention this evening. Is she your mistress?" Miranda smirked.

Adrian's brow rose. "Not that such a subject should be discussed with you, but do you in all honesty think I would bring my mistress to our sister's wedding?"

Miranda sighed. "I suppose not. They make a lovely couple, do they not?"

"Gracie and Nicholas will have many happy years ahead of them," he concurred, not paying the least bit of attention to them.

Miranda laughed. "Not the newly wedded couple, silly. I meant Celia and Phillip."

"Phillip? When did you become on a first-name basis with the Marquis?"

"You may as well get on a first-name basis with him too, brother, if he allows it," Miranda replied with a flip of her head and an irritating smirk on her face.

"Why?" he asked in morbid curiosity.

Miranda feigned shock. "Why, have you not heard the rumors, Adrian?"

His brow rose, wondering what his devious little sister was up to now. "Heard what news?"

"The news that Lady Celia and Wyndham are all but engaged, of course! Have you been hiding under a rock to not hear the whisperings within the *ton*? Her parents and his thoroughly approve of the match. I expect an announcement to hit the post any day and am surprised it has not shown up as yet."

Miranda continued chatting away, but to Adrian, her words vanished away while he watched the subject of their discussion laugh up into her partner's face. Celia appeared radiant until their gazes once more met across the space between them. Surely Adrian did not imagine the longing reflected there. In that one instant, he knew Celia was still in love with him. How, then, was she to marry another, and more importantly, did he care enough to attempt to change her mind?

CHAPTER 3

C elia ran her fingers along several spines before she pulled a volume that looked interesting from the bookshelf. A gasp escaped her when she stared at the face now exposed on the opposite side.

"Good heavens, Lord de Courtenay... you gave me a fright," she said in a breathy whisper of disbelief. He was so close. His blue eyes twinkled mischievously as though he was pleased to see her so flustered, despite the fact there was a whole shelf separating them. She replaced the tome, hiding him from her vision, and turned around to inspect the shelf behind her.

She caught a glimpse of him as he rounded the corner of the darkened section of the aisle. He was apparently in no hurry to move past her, for he casually leaned one shoulder against the shelf. He took his time while he inspected her, or so it seemed when she watched him from the corner of her eye.

"Hello, Celia," he murmured, and the silky tone of his voice almost caused her knees to buckle. Almost... such a reaction would never do!

She turned, giving him a short curtsey before she returned her attention to the books in front of her, not that she could even focus on their titles. "My lord," Celia managed. "Whatever brings you here?" She almost banged her head against the wood frame in front of her. *Why did anyone go to a bookshop, you fool!*

His long fingers pulled at the nearest volume, but he did not take his eyes from her, so she knew he cared not for the contents of whatever book he now held.

"I was in need of something new to read," he said, before tucking the tome close to his chest.

A sense of *déjà vu* filled Celia and reminded her of her recklessness while at Hollystone. "I was looking for something as well," she explained, taking the first book closest to her fingertips.

A chuckle escaped lips she was certain would take her to the stars if he would but kiss her. He stepped forward to examine her choice. "A medical journal, Celia?" he laughed. "I would have thought you more inclined to a romance or the very least something by Shakespeare."

Her chin rose. "I needed something stimulating."

"And you think you will find such between the pages of some boring medical book?" he asked with a raised brow, obviously amused by her answer.

"You think me incapable of understanding the text."

Her words were a statement. He was either not impressed or knew she had no desire to read anything in the book she held.

"I would never imply such a thing, dear lady. I only mention it because I would find myself napping before I even managed to make it through the introduction."

"To each their own, my lord," she chided. "Is that not how the saying goes?"

"Yes... I suppose it is," he replied, stepping even closer. "Hopefully, you enjoy the written word within."

His cologne reached her senses, and she did everything within her power not to sigh in pleasure. The scent reminded her of spices and mulled wine all wrapped up into the very essence that seemed to be all Adrian, and he had no idea what he did to her emotions with his nearness.

She raised her eyes and saw his amusement twinkling in the depths of those blue orbs. The rogue! He knew exactly what he was doing to her, but Celia had no idea as to his intentions. He was possibly interested in her, and yet he had made it clear he did not want to pursue the matter. Perhaps, her age still mattered to him. Her birthday was still several months away. Nevertheless... She could not miss his flirtatious glances in her direction but was flirting all he intended? What exactly was she to him? A mild distraction? Celia had no idea.

"Is Lady Sarah with you today?" *Where the hell had those words come from?* They just seemed to tumble from her mouth of their own accord. His smirk told her many things must be going on inside that handsome head of his. Confidence? Without any doubt. Celia was sure her attraction to him must be clearly written all over her face. She was never very good at hiding her feelings from Adrian. Arrogance about his own good looks? Most likely... surely, he knew how handsome he was. Why, any woman in her right mind would be following him to get his attention. Yet, here he was with her, practically alone in this darkened section of the store.

"No, Celia. Lady Sarah is not with me today. I actually accompanied my sister, Miranda."

Celia looked around him, expecting Miranda to suddenly appear. "How lovely. I should love to speak to her. I have not seen her since the wedding."

"I am not sure if I care for you to spend much time with my sister," he answered, a scowl crossing his brow.

Celia did her best to hide her surprise. "I was not aware your sister was unsuitable company. Surely you do not hold that ghastly event at Hollystone against her."

He swore beneath his breath. "My apologies. I indeed have the highest regard for my sister. It is only the mischievous side to her nature that I am against. I would not wish for you to fall prey to one of her outlandish ideas or the bets she tends to concoct in her pretty little head."

"You do your sister a disservice to think only the worst of her. I found her quite entertaining and a delight to converse with," Celia replied.

Adrian held his hands up as though in surrender, then laughed. "Do not let it be said I did not try to warn you. I have tried to curb her marital ambitions and to ensure she does not make a fool of herself again in front of the whole of Society. But Miranda cannot seem to keep from diving into the middle of situations she should not be near in the first place."

"You should have more confidence in her, my lord," Celia replied, standing up for her friend. "Maybe she feels alone in the world with her older sister married twice now and Miranda as yet unwed."

"I see my sister has a mighty champion in her corner," Adrian said, with another heart stopping grin.

"It is obvious someone needs to stand up for her. Her brother certainly does not," Celia huffed.

"I stand corrected, little one." The endearment slipped from his lips, and he seemed surprised by it. He cleared his throat. "I will, in the future, endeavor to see another side to my sister."

"I shall hold you to that oath, my lord," Celia said, pointing her finger at him.

He reached for her hand before bowing low over her knuckles. His breath through her glove warmed her, and she could tell her cheeks glowed from the attention he was bestowing upon her.

"You have my word, Celia," he replied, and yet he still held her hand. His thumb moved back and forth in a soft caress, and she tried not to moan as butterflies flitted inside her belly. He at last realized what he was doing, and he let her hand fall while his other hand clutched the book closer to his chest. "I never did ask. Are you also here with your sisters?"

His interest in her delighted her and scattered her wits so she had to scramble to remember who else was with her this day. "Yes, I am, as a matter of fact. Elinor and Alice are somewhere about," she waved her hand in the air. "We are also accompanied by— "

"There you are, Lady Celia," the marquis called out, coming to her side. "Your sisters asked me to search for you. Are you ready to depart? They are eager to continue our ride through Hyde Park."

Phillip and Adrian began speaking with one another as they introduced themselves. Inwardly, Celia cringed. The marquis was a nice man, but he was not Adrian. She and the marquis had gone out on several occasions since her uncle's marriage, but as far as Celia's heart was concerned, there just was no spark between them. Not like with Adrian.

Phillip held out his arm. "Shall we, Lady Celia?"

"Yes, of course. We should not keep the rest of our party waiting," Celia answered. She put the book back onto the shelf and took Phillip's arm. "May you enjoy the rest of your day, Lord de Courtenay."

"It was a pleasure conversing with you again, *my* lady," he murmured with a bow.

Her heart skipped a beat hearing the emphasis on him calling her his lady, and his words continued to stay with her when she left the book shop without anything new to read.

As Phillip assisted her into their waiting carriage, Celia stared at the window where Adrian now kept vigil. She turned her attention back to Phillip once he sat next to her, and he began conversing with her sisters who laughed at his joke. Celia must have missed the part of the conversation that made what he was saying funny. What was she doing with him anyway? Damn Miranda and her big ideas to use him as a way to make Adrian jealous!

CHAPTER 4

Adrian looked up from the morning paper to see his brother-in-law in the foyer at White's. Folding the paper, Adrian took out his watch fob and consulted the time, wondering how it was now well into the afternoon. He motioned for a passing servant to bring two brandies to the table and waited for Nicholas to be seated.

Adrian pushed the paper away and reached for his drink once it was delivered. He raised the crystal in a silent salute. "Good to see you out of your town house, Nicholas. Is Gracie driving you mad yet?" he laughed, taking a sip of his drink.

"Eh gads, Adrian, do you think me such a cad as to actually say such a thing about my wife? " Nicholas exclaimed, sipping his drink. "I am a happily married man. Life is good, as you yourself will one day learn once you find a woman of your own whom you cannot do without."

Adrian tried hard not to envision the young lady with blonde hair and bright blue eyes who was the niece of the man before him. "I have yet to come across such a paragon of virtue that I would give up my single status," Adrian replied dryly.

"Maybe you are not looking hard enough."

"Maybe I am not looking at all. There is no hurry for me to change my current situation. In the meantime, I have a mistress to see to my needs."

"A mistress is not the same as a wife."

Adrian chuckled. "A mistress is better. I come and go as I please and visit her when I want. A wife would surely be more demanding of my time."

"But not as satisfying," Nicholas retaliated.

"Maybe you never had the right mistress," Adrian joked.

Nicholas tried to hold down his laughter and failed. "I have no desire to go down that road again. Gracie would have my head served on a platter if I ever had the briefest thought of straying to another woman."

"Rightly so," Adrian murmured. "I would hate to call you out if you hurt her, by the way."

Nicholas held up his hands. "I would provide you the pistol myself, Adrian, if such a ridiculous notion ever crossed my mind. As I said, I am completely and insanely in love with my wife. Never been happier..."

"Imagine... actually being in love with one's wife. What a concept."

"Surely, you must have your eye set on someone, Adrian. At some point you will need to produce an heir so your line does not die out."

Adrian nodded before taking another sip of his drink, trying hard not to envision Celia as his bride. "When would I have had time to fall in love? If I do not hold my distance, all the marriage-minded mothers and their daughters would be on me like a pack of wolves. It is hard enough as it is. I do not dare take a moment in a garden or a withdrawing room, for fear of some would-be countess leaping out of a corner and ending up with my ring on her finger."

Nicholas shook his head. "As bad as that, eh?"

Adrian changed the subject. "How is your family since you have wed? Do they miss your sparkling conversation?"

"My brother and his duchess are taking to their countryside estate. She has been unwell, and he hopes the fresh air might do her some good, considering her delicate condition."

"Ah, I see," Adrian replied in an attempt to not appear too anxious to hear news of Celia, Nicholas's youngest niece. Yet he could not help himself. "Will your nieces join them?"

"The eldest, Elinor, will join them shortly. She had some business that needed attending to, most likely from another one of her *causes*. Alice and Celia are already on their way."

"Celia has left London?" he asked before common sense returned to him, and he cleared his throat to cover his mistake. "I mean, I just saw her the other day."

Nicholas peered at him briefly before continuing on. "Celia wished to travel with her mother, or so I was told, as did Alice. Their whole household is in a complete upheaval as they make arrangements to open the house in Langridge near Bath."

"I have a smaller estate outside there as well, in Saltford. And is not Highgrove Manor close by?"

"Yes, in Batheaston. My brother has now charged me with opening my own house in order that we may host a celebration for Celia's upcoming birthday. Grace is thrilled for the opportunity to entertain. And I would never disappoint my niece by telling my brother to host his own damn party. You should be sure to attend, being family and all..."

"Celia will be ten and seven?" he inquired while swirling the amber liquid in the crystal glassware.

Nicolas chuckled. "Ten and eight, and do not let Celia know you thought of her as younger. That young woman is so damn anxious to grow up it near breaks my heart."

"She is to wed soon?" Adrian asked with a clenched jaw. Thoughts of Celia in the arms of Wyndham almost choked the air from his lungs.

"Whatever gave you that idea?" Nicholas asked with a scowl.

Miranda's whisperings rushed across his mind. "Rumor has it the Marquis of Wyndham has asked for her hand in marriage."

"Damn it to hell!" Nicholas swore. "Does Society have nothing better to do than to gossip about a well-bred young lady?"

Adrian's brow rose. "You should know they do not. The rumors are not true?"

"Not that I am aware of, but then I have not been much interested in what my niece has been up to, since I've been too busy enjoying married life." Nicholas took another drink, then set his glass down to peer at him. "Celia would make any man an exceptional wife."

Adrian laughed. "She is barely out of the schoolroom."

Nicholas shrugged. "Some would say she, along with her sisters, are already on the shelf. Why my brother will not agree to any of the proposals for their hands is beyond me."

"Maybe the duke knows his daughter's suitors only see what they will gain monetarily rather than the women themselves."

Nicholas nodded. "Foolish men, all of them, if such is the case. My nieces are true diamonds. Gems... every one of them and that most definitely includes Celia."

"She is a lovely young lady," Adrian murmured, lifting his glass to his lips.

"Maybe you should offer for her," Nicholas suggested.

Adrian almost spewed his brandy and began choking on the drink instead. "Why me?" he at last gasped out.

Nicholas chuckled. "Why *not* you? You do not care for her?"

"I barely know her," Adrian said, wondering how this conversation had gotten so out of hand.

"Perhaps you should change that."

"But we are already family," Adrian retorted.

"Only by marriage and no one would take you to task if you developed an affection for her."

"I feel as though you are pawning your niece off on me."

"I never said such a thing. I only made the suggestion and gave you a possible thought about a lady to take to wife. What you do with such information is entirely up to you."

"I am not ready to wed," Adrian grumbled, draining the remainder of his drink.

Nicholas laughed. "I will ensure you receive an invitation, not that Grace would forget to invite her own brother to the first party where she will act as hostess. You will have no better time to become further acquainted with my niece than at a celebration for her birthday. Shall we play cards?" Nicholas stood and took his drink as he left the table.

Adrian muttered something beneath his breath but followed his brother-in-law into the card room, where he was soundly trounced when he paid no attention to his bet and what he actually held in his hand.

He left White's shortly thereafter and found himself across town staring up at the windows of the house belonging to his mistress, Mrs. Josephine Bouchard. A down-on-her-luck widow, she had quickly agreed to an arrangement that suited them both. She was in need of a protector and someone to pay for her household and personal expenses. He was in need of someone to fulfill his baser needs. Josephine was undemanding of his time and that was the way he liked to keep their relationship.

He hesitated for several minutes before he made his way up the steps and used the knocker. Josephine opened the door herself, and her face lit up with happiness when she saw him.

"Adrian! What a pleasant surprise," she said, wrapping her arms around his neck once the door closed behind him. "It has been forever since I have seen you."

He chuckled. "It has hardly been that long, my dear. Have I come at a bad time?" he asked, knowing he did not. Josephine was just what he needed for the moment. He began pulling the pins from her dark brown hair, and it fell to her waist in a silky display of curls.

Her laughter filled the foyer. "Of course not. I am just surprised to see you here in the middle of the afternoon." Soft brown eyes stared back at him even while he tried not to think of another. Adrian watched her lips turn up into a welcoming smile.

He pulled her close and ran a finger along her cheek,

inhaling the flowery scent of her hair. "Make me forget…" he whispered into her ear, before he began to kiss her. There was no need for further words between them, and she took his hand to lead him into her bedroom.

Adrian spent the rest of the afternoon pleasing his mistress, but in the early hours of the morning, as he stared up at the ceiling in his own bedroom, he began to feel as though he had betrayed another. Why? They made no commitment to one another. Celia had only thus far been a mild flirtation. So why, then, did he feel so guilty?

CHAPTER 5

The Duke of Ashbury's Country Estate
Autumn, 1813

Celia tugged on her gloves while she made her way to her mother's bedroom. Reaching the door, she knocked and, at the call to enter, pushed open the portal. Her mother sat in a chair near the window with Elinor and Alice by her side.

As Celia strode across the room, she took a shawl from a servant and placed the wrap over her mother's shoulders. Kneeling down, Celia placed her hand on her mother's stomach.

"How is my little sister or brother treating you this evening, Mother?" Celia asked with a worried frown. Her mother looked pale, and it was no wonder. She was expected to give birth in the next month.

The duchess waved her hand in the air. "You three

must stop fussing over me. I am perfectly well, and you should be on your way to your uncle's instead of attending me."

Elinor leaned down to place a kiss on their mother's cheek. "We cannot help but worry over you, Mother. It hardly seems proper to leave you here alone while we go out and pretend to enjoy a party without you."

Her mother gasped. "Oh, but I insist," she said. "Celia deserves to have a lovely party to celebrate her birthday."

Alice took her hand. "I can stay behind," she suggested with a slight smile.

The duchess shook her head. "I will not hear of it." Her tone told them more than anything else she could have said.

Alice stood, but as she glanced between them, Celia could see how worried she was about their mother's condition. What were they not telling her?

Celia laid her head on her mother's lap. "We should have cancelled the party," Celia murmured, her lip quivered in concern over her mother's health.

The duchess reached down to caress Celia's cheek. "Do not be silly, my darling girl. I will be fine, as I have told you all before. I insist you go and enjoy this evening. Your uncle and aunt have gone to a great deal of effort to open their house in time to hold this event on my behalf. I would hate to disappoint them if their main reason for having a party does not plan to attend," she said with a smile.

Celia sighed and forced a smile to her lips. "Of course, Mother. I would hate to disappoint you, Uncle Nicholas, or Aunt Grace."

"That's my girl. Besides, I have something for you." The duchess smiled, waving her hand towards a servant who brought forth a wrapped box.

Celia accepted the present and tore open the wrapping paper. Inside was a tiara studded with diamonds and sapphires. "Oh Mother... this is too much," Celia exclaimed even though she was dying to try it on.

Caroline laughed. "Do not be silly. Every young woman should wear a tiara on her birthday, and this once belonged to your great-grandmother. She would be pleased to see you wearing it tonight, since it matches your dress."

Lifting the small tiara from the bed of velvet, Celia went to her mother's vanity, and a maid secured it around her hair. She could hardly believe that the woman staring back at her was no longer a young girl fresh out of the schoolroom. She squared her shoulders, still gazing at her reflection. She was a woman full grown and ready to fall in love.

Celia heard her sisters' giggles behind her and turned in her chair. "Whatever are you two so amused about?" she huffed, thinking they were about to make fun of her as they did in their youth. She had always been the baby of the family and the darling of her mother's eye. With a new sibling expecting to arrive soon, Celia had a brief moment of jealousy and wondered if this new child would take her place in her mother's eyes.

Alice clapped her hands. "The marquis is going to be more in love with you than he already is once he sees you tonight."

The marquis... Phillip had been a delight, escorting her to any event she wished to attend while in London. While it had been Miranda's idea to use the marquis to make Adrian jealous, Celia had quickly come to the realization that she could not stoop so low. She had told Miranda she would no longer attempt to use such a ruse, for it would benefit no one. It was unfair to Phillip and certainly unfair to Adrian, not that she saw him enough to make such a difference.

Unfortunately, all her thoughts of using Phillip came to backfire on her when her father, in particular, favored him. But in her heart, she knew she would never come to love Phillip. Was not love important in a marriage? Her gaze fell to her mother, reflected in the mirror as she watched her daughter. Her parents' marriage was *manageable*, she surmised, for her father was a difficult man to get along with, and her mother suffered for it. Celia supposed in his heart he loved her mother and the daughters she had produced, but none of them were an heir to carry on his lofty title and name. If this next child was not a son, then, upon her father's death, his title would revert to her Uncle Nicholas.

She pulled herself from her sudden melancholy mood when her father came to the bedroom door as though Celia had conjured the man up from her thoughts.

He peered into the doorway. "Well? Are you three ready? We are late." He pulled out his watch fob to inspect the time before placing it back into his jacket.

No smile. No happy birthday wishes. Just a simple statement of irritation that they were not already in the carriage awaiting his esteemed presence. Celia should be used to his coldness by now. One would think he would have the decency to offer at least a few kind words to his daughter on her special day.

Celia waited another moment in the hopes he might say a kind word or two to her, but he only held the door wide so they could leave her mother's room. She gave a heavy sigh. "We are ready, Father," she murmured before going quickly back to her mother to place a quick kiss upon her upturned face. "Thank you for the present. It is beautiful."

The duchess smiled and reached up to cup her face. "It is only a piece of jewelry, my dearest. *You* are what is beautiful, today and every day. Never forget how much I love you."

"I love you, too, Mother," she whispered, thankful that at least one of her parents adored her.

Her father cleared his throat, giving a clear indication that his patience was at an end. He gave a brief bow to her mother before he quit the room, his footsteps echoing in the hall as he left.

Celia and her sisters rushed to catch up to him.

Grabbing their wraps at the door, they quickly entered the carriage, and they had barely taken their seat before the horses were put into motion. The ride to her uncle's country estate did not take long; the property was near their own but still on the outskirts of Bath. The manor was impressive, and Celia peered out the window to see the row of carriages also just arriving.

When their conveyance came to a stop at the front door, her father held her back while her sisters left the carriage. Celia smiled at him, thinking he would at last have a few kind words for her. She should not have been surprised when he did not.

"You should continue to spend time with the Marquis of Wyndham. He will make you an exceptional husband and see you are kept in a manner appropriate to your standing as my daughter." His voice was flat and held no emotion whatsoever; a monotone of indifference that caused Celia's heart to lurch in her chest.

"Of course, Father," she hastily choked out, and without another word to her, he left her sitting there alone while he entered his brother's home.

Celia quickly composed herself and squared her shoulders. This was *her* party, and no one, not even her father, was going to ruin it! She set a smile upon her face, entered her uncle's home, and promptly searched for the one man who already had stolen her heart.

CHAPTER 6

Adrian accepted a flute of champagne from a passing servant while his gaze followed the woman who occupied more of his thoughts than she should. Why he had an attraction to such a young slip of a girl... or woman, he could not say. But she held his interest, though he would not admit such to her—or to anyone else for that matter.

"She is lovely, is she not?" His sister Grace linked her arm through his, and he noticed how she, too, watched Lady Celia while she laughed with a group of her friends.

Lovely indeed, he thought, consumed suddenly by the urge to feel her silken hair running through his fingers as he took the pins from her coiffure. He thought of the small gift for her that he had in his jacket and wondered when he would have the opportunity to present it to her.

"Adrian..." His sister whispered, then tugged on his arm, pulling him from his musings. She peered at him with a peculiar twinkle in her eyes.

He cleared his throat before taking a sip of his champagne. "Yes," he finally answered. "Lady Celia looks beautiful tonight. It was kind of you and Nicholas to host her birthday party."

"Her mother is unwell," Grace confided in a hushed tone. "The pregnancy has taken its toll on the duchess."

His brow rose. "I was unaware her health was in such a serious condition, not that we should be discussing such an issue."

"We are all family. I suppose it did not occur to me that I should remain silent."

"I hope the duchess will return to good health once she has delivered," he replied, keeping his voice hushed, before turning his attention back to the reason why he was at Highgrove Manor in the first place. Adrian could not seem to take his eyes from Lady Celia, but when Wyndham came to whisper in the woman's ear, causing her to laugh, a scowl crossed his brow.

"I understand the duke favors him," Grace said, as though she knew where his thoughts had wandered, "that is, unless someone else who is equally her match comes along to steal her heart."

Adrian's own gaze traveled down to his sister, who was peering up at him expectedly. "You cannot possibly be thinking that I am her match?"

Grace laughed. "She would make you an exceptional wife. Why should you not pursue her, if you favor her?"

"I never said I favored her," Adrian replied, scoffing at the idea of laying claim to the lady when her father already approved of another.

"You did not have to, Adrian. Your face, while you watch her, tells me more than anything you could say. Take a chance and see if you have a common accord."

"I am nine years older than her—"

"—and your age has nothing to do with anything. Admit it," Grace prodded as though she was jabbing him with a stick, "you like her, no matter her age."

He watched Wyndham escort Lady Celia toward the ballroom, and something inside Adrian lurched. He did indeed care for the lady. But if the duke was already expecting a match for his daughter with a marquis, then a mere earl would hardly be a better choice.

He drained his glass and handed the flute to another passing servant. "I am hardly in the position to be on the same playing field as the marquis. As you very well know, the only reason I have a title at all is because your first husband, God rest his soul, passed away and left you childless."

Grace jerked her arm from his and squared her shoulders. "Thank you, *brother*, for that kind reminder." Her fan snapped open as she began to frantically wave it to cover her face while unshed tears formed in her eyes.

Adrian pulled her close. "My apologies, Gracie, for

being so thoughtless. I am a complete buffoon. Forgive me?" he asked, taking her free hand and caressing it with his thumb.

"I still miss him in many ways," Grace murmured, "but am thankful that I had a second chance to fall in love."

"I am happy for you, Gracie," Adrian replied and watched his sister's face light up when her husband began to cross the room. "Nicholas is lucky to have you, as well."

Grace looked up into Adrian's eyes. She squeezed his arm. "And I want you to be just as happy. Find Lady Celia. Dance with her. I know she favors you above all others and would welcome the chance to get to know you better."

"She said this to you?" he asked, surprised.

Grace's smile reached her eyes. "She did not have to, either, Adrian."

He had no time to reply before Grace was escorted toward the dance floor by her husband. Adrian moved in the direction of the ballroom as though some unseen force pulled him toward the room... no... not the room. He went because Lady Celia was there, even though she danced with another. He might as well be honest with himself and admit that something about the young lady pulled him toward her.

Adrian watched the lady's footwork while she performed the lively pattern of the dance. She was an exceptional dancer as was her current partner. The music ended, and the dancers began to clap. He watched when Wyndham excused himself from Lady Celia, leaving Adrian a prime opportunity to converse with her.

He lessened the distance between them. Her back was towards him, but she suddenly turned to almost land directly in his arms, as if she had felt his presence.

"Adrian…" Her voice was a breathy whisper. Her smile lit her entire face causing even her eyes to sparkle with delight.

He gave a short bow, pleased with her reaction. "Lady Celia. I have not had the chance to offer you best wishes on your birthday. How lovely you look tonight, my lady," he said, wondering why his heart was hammering in his chest as though she was the first lady he had ever spoken to.

She curtseyed. "Thank you, my lord. I am so happy you could join us this evening. It was kind of your sister and my uncle to open their home for the occasion."

"I am certain they were more than happy to do so."

"Are you enjoying yourself thus far?" she asked, smiling up at him again.

He returned her smile with one of his own. "I am now," he replied and watched how pleased she was with his answer. "I know I should not ask to take you away from your guests, but might you join me for a moment on the balcony?"

She gasped, her hand reaching for her throat. "Alone?"

"I promise we shall remain in sight so no one can question that I was anything but a gentleman," he vowed, offering his arm.

Celia hesitated but briefly, before her gloved hand made its way into the crook of his arm. "As long as we remain near the open door. I would not wish to give my father reason to..." her words drifted off as though she was wary of how much she should say.

"Upon my honor, you shall be perfectly safe with me. We are, after all, family."

You idiot! Those were hardly the words he intended, and he saw her face fall in disappointment even while he cursed himself for his stupidity. If he was going to give in to the reality that she meant something to him, the last thing he wanted was the grim reminder that they were, in fact, related by marriage.

The balcony doors had been left open to let in the cooler air of the night, making the terrace a welcoming refuge from a warm room overflowing with guests. It was one of those mild autumn evenings when one could forget that winter would soon sweep across the land. Still, Adrian watched Celia shiver when they reached the terrace railing. He hoped the reaction was from his nearness and not from actually being cold.

Celia turned to face him, a look of apprehension lighting her face while her eyes continued to scan the ballroom. "What did you wish to speak about, my lord?" she asked, getting straight to the reason for leaving the ballroom.

He quickly got to his point, wondering what she was so concerned about that her eyes continued to search for something inside. Perhaps she wished to return to Wyndham. Shaking that thought aside, he gave his answer. "I have a gift for the birthday girl," he said with a grin, before reaching inside his jacket to retrieve the small velvet box.

Her brow quirked upwards. "I am hardly a girl anymore, Adrian," she whispered. She accepted his offering, running her thumb over the lid.

"Yes, of course. A woman full grown with all Society at her feet," he teased her.

A small laugh escaped her. "I hardly doubt all of the *ton* are waiting for me with open arms, my lord, and certainly they will not be at my beck and call."

"Come now... a beautiful young woman such as you will have a line of beaus in no time waiting to escort you about town once you return to London for the next season."

Her gaze wandered once more to the room full of guests. "Not if my father has anything to say on the matter," she murmured.

Her sad expression gave him pause. He did not wish to be the cause of ruining her party. "Enough of all that for now. I refuse to see anything else but a smile upon your face. Will you not open my gift?"

She laughed, and this time, the sound was pleasing to his ears. "Oh yes... your gift." Celia gave one more look at him before she flicked open the lid to the box. Her eyes widened when she saw the necklace; a small golden bird frozen in flight. "It is beautiful."

"It is but a trifle. When I saw this in the local jewelers, I thought of you," Adrian said.

"You did?"

Her breathy tone made him smile. Looking into her eyes, Adrian paused to stare. Were those unshed tears he saw lingering upon her lashes? One would think he had presented the young woman with diamonds and rubies, considering her reaction to such a small trinket.

He took the box from her hands, pulling the necklace from the silken lining. "May I?" he offered, holding out the jewelry so she might wear it?

"Oh, yes, please," she exclaimed, not hiding the excitement from her voice. "It is lovely, Adrian. Thank you so much for my gift."

She turned around so he could fasten the clasp around her neck. He fumbled with the chain when the floral scent of Celia's hair, along with the faint touch of her perfume, assaulted his senses. After he at last put the necklace in place, he took but a brief moment to stare in wonder at her creamy skin, the smallness of her waist. A sudden urge to pull her into his arms was suppressed only when the lady swiftly swung around and took hold of his hands.

Adrian was surprised at the gesture, and even more

so when she quickly leaned up on her toes to bestow a short kiss upon his cheek. A fleeting moment etched in time as though they were the only two people in the world, and the rest of Society and her party no longer mattered.

CHAPTER 7

Her impulse to bend forward to kiss Adrian's cheek may have been an innocent enough gesture in her mind, yet her heart apparently thought differently, given its rapid rhythm. Could he hear the staccato sound that betrayed her feelings for him whether she voiced them aloud or not? Surely he could, since he was standing so close. Was she the only one who felt as though the world was tipping, as if his mere presence made her head spin?

She *should* step away. She *should* distance herself from the man who caused such reckless behavior. She *should* mumble an apology and flee into the ballroom as fast as her slippered feet could carry her.

Yet here she stood, even daring to step closer when she felt the slightest pull from Adrian's hand on her elbow. It was so subtle that Celia could easily mistake such a harmless touch as nothing. Instead, she hoped he desired her closer. Her reaction to the gift may have been her undoing. She was unsure her heart could stand much more.

He took several steps backward, plunging himself into the shadows of the night but not releasing her hand. Fool that she was, Celia willingly followed his lead. Not caring she was no longer in sight of those who may be watching, her spirits soared knowing Adrian... yes, Adrian... wanted to steal a few moments alone together.

Had she not dreamed of this moment for months since they were first introduced at Hollystone Hall? His sister Miranda's words that Celia should make Adrian jealous in order to win him were but a small memory. She had told Miranda months ago that she could not resort to such a ploy and such unladylike behavior was not becoming of a genteel lady. Miranda had laughed, telling Celia sometimes harsh measures were needed in order to obtain what the heart desired.

Clearly such foolery had not been necessary, because here she was with Adrian. He led her into the dark of his own accord and not because she made him jealous with another. A brief glimpse of the marquis flashed in her mind, but she brushed away the image of his face, knowing she had made no commitment to the man despite her father's wishes. Phillip did not own her heart, and he never would. It belonged to Adrian from the first moment she had seen him.

Lost in her thoughts, Celia realized they had not

gone far, and for that, she was grateful. She could still easily make a hasty escape if necessary, especially if they heard someone approaching.

Adrian gently maneuvered her against the brick of the manor in the shelter of a trellis filled with ivy vines. He placed his body as a protective shield so she was efficiently hidden. Her mind worked furiously. Had he done this before with some other willing lady? Was she just another conquest?

His long fingers reached out and took her chin, tilting her face upward so she could do nothing more than stare into those mesmerizing blue eyes. The corners of his mouth lifted into a sensual grin, and Celia was lost to everything but him.

"Adrian..."

She blurted his name as though they were already lovers and felt a blush color her face crimson. She hoped he could not see it in the dim light. Her hands moved of their own accord to tentatively touch his waist. At her apparent encouragement, he stepped even closer until she could feel the very heat of him against her young trembling body. His hand slid to her cheek; the thumb rubbed a gentle pattern as if to calm her, but she was anything but calm. The anticipation of his kiss was going to kill her.

A heavy sigh escaped him. "You should leave." His voice was strained as though he was struggling within himself.

"Yes... I probably should." Her hands crept upward

to finger the buttons of his waistcoat, the floral pattern in deep contrast to the rest of his dark attire. A mental image from her dreams of undressing Adrian on their wedding night startled her, and she quickly shifted her hands to the edge of his jacket as if holding onto him might give her strength and the support she needed to remain level headed.

His breath was warm against her temple when he placed a soft kiss at her hairline before he touched his forehead to her own.

"You are not leaving," he murmured, his hands moving down her arms as if she needed warming. His voice was low and husky, causing her flesh to shiver in anticipation of the unknown.

"I cannot," she managed to croak out, while she tried to find a way to breathe. Somewhere in the recesses of her mind she knew she must flee, but she ignored the warning, especially when her stomach flipped as his arm swooped around her waist.

"Why not?" he asked, pulling her closer so there was no doubt left in her mind that he wanted her. She may be young, but she certainly understood the fundamentals of what might happen when she took the hand of a rake and plunged into the coolness of the night.

Celia wound her arms around his neck, touching the curling edges of his brown hair. God only knew how much she had been dying to do that since Hollystone Hall. She swallowed hard and rushed onward, her fate sealed to this man whether he knew it or not. "Because

I have dreamed of your kisses from the day we first met," she confessed, her words louder than she intended, as though such an admission should be shouted for all the world to hear.

Adrian muttered something beneath his breath before he gave her a little shake. "I made you a promise I would behave as a gentleman," he growled. But he did not let her go, and his face showed an internal struggle.

His voice made her shiver yet again, but she kept her place within his embrace. "I would expect nothing less."

He took her face into the palms of his hands in order to study her reaction to his touch. She covered one of his hands with her own. "If we stay out here, I have no doubt I will break my vow," he replied.

"Then, before I lose my nerve to ask you..." Celia hesitated only an instant before she rushed on in an urgent plea, "...kiss me, Adrian. Kiss me like—"

...*you love me*, she finished inside her head when he cut off her words; for she could not speak when Adrian did just that. Kissed her. Right there. In the moonlight. With half of Society but a breath away.

His kiss was demanding at first. She had no idea what to do with her mouth, since this was her very first kiss. He must have realized that fact because everything changed between them. He softened his lips on hers as he possessed her mouth, but still, their situation was charged with an unseen energy that Celia never wanted to end.

Unsure what to do, she at first stood as still as one of the marble statues in her uncle's garden. A gentle urging from Adrian encouraged her to open her mouth and follow his lead. A willing pupil, she allowed the master to teach her what he enjoyed, and she discovered that she enjoyed it, too.

He easily slipped his tongue inside. Warm fire erupted in her veins, while her tongue tangled with his. A low moan escaped her, unbidden but easily detected in the silence of the night. A tell-tale sign of the true depth of her feelings for the man who kissed her senseless.

Nothing had ever prepared her for the heady rush of sensations that enveloped her whole being. His arms tightened around her. She clutched him as if she was starving and only Adrian could satisfy her cravings. Nothing mattered. Not the ball. Not her sisters. Not Phillip. Not even her father. If Adrian could kiss her like this, then surely he, too, must care for her. *Did he love...?*

"Celia!"

They tore their lips apart as the sound of her name continued to echo off into the night. Her breathing heavy, she melted into Adrian's arms, placing her head upon his chest while she heard his own heartbeat running wild. He was just as affected as she was.

"You must go," he insisted, pulling her from his embrace and straightening his jacket.

She gave him a pout and saw his brow rise in amusement. "I wish to stay here with you."

"And I refuse to ruin your reputation, especially today of all days. Imagine if we are caught outside and you without a chaperone."

"I do not care..."

"...and I care enough for the both of us. Now go." Adrian gave her a small push. "I will return to the ballroom from a different direction."

She stood her ground. "We should talk about—"

"Go!" Adrian urged before taking her hand and giving it a quick kiss.

"C-Celia..." Miranda's voice drew out Celia's name in a singsong like pattern. Good heavens! Did the musicians have to pick just that moment to finish playing their tune?

Silence descended upon the night, startling Celia into action. "Promise me you shall ask me to dance," Celia murmured. "It *is* my birthday, after all."

"Yes. I promise. Now, go, before my sister ruins everything." He gave her another push, and Celia took flight. She looked back only once before she rounded the corner of the manor, but Adrian had already disappeared into the night.

The lit balcony came into her view, and there was Miranda hugging Phillip's arm. Odd that. Celia frowned, wondering what ploy Miranda was up to now. Miranda appeared startled when Celia stepped from the shadows.

"There she is, my lord," Miranda beamed, "and none the worse for wear, it appears."

"I needed a breath of fresh air. I felt faint," Celia replied, coming up to the pair.

Phillip stepped back as though she was about to embarrass herself by actually getting sick in front of him. "You are unwell?" he inquired politely.

Miranda continued her possession of the marquis's arm as though she belonged there. "You do looked a bit flushed, my dear. Are you sure you should not, perhaps, lie down to rest?"

Was that hope ringing in her tone? Celia could only guess what the woman was about, but Miranda would in no way ruin her party. She had a dance with Adrian to look forward to.

Celia laughed off Miranda's comment. "Nonsense. I am perfectly fine. As I said, I just needed a bit of air, but I am feeling myself again. Shall we rejoin the party?"

Celia did not bother to wait for an answer, but instead, went inside. If Miranda wanted to pursue a relationship with Phillip, then she could have him. Celia's heart had already been stolen by an earl who entered from the opposite side of the ballroom. Adrian gave her a silent toast with a half empty glass of champagne. Now, if only he would declare his love...

CHAPTER 8

Adrian swallowed the last of his champagne in one gulp, wishing it was something stronger, something with a bite to fortify him against this overwhelming desire to pull Wyndham away from Celia. Celia... who appeared completely bored while the marquis escorted her toward the buffet table. He watched her intently as she took a flute of champagne before searching the room... *for him*. He had no doubt about whom she was looking for, because when their eyes connected, even from this distance, he could see her light up in sparkling fascination.

He began moving closer, and he swore she blushed before she averted her eyes so he could no longer determine her mood. Not that he could not guess. He, too, was just as affected by their little encounter. It had gone far out of hand. He had never intended to kiss Celia, but he certainly did not regret doing so either.

Adrian watched as her father approached her and briefly whispered in her ear. Suddenly, she appeared as skittish as a newborn colt. Whatever the duke had said to his daughter, it had clearly upset her, for her face no longer showed the happiness it held but moments before.

He cared not what anyone thought as he approached her. He cared not that Miranda seemed to be smirking as if she actually knew what had happened out on the balcony. He cared not that the duke's eyebrows drew together, his mouth a thin line of displeasure. Nor did he care one jot that Wyndham stepped forward to block Adrian's view of Celia.

Adrian stepped around the marquis and held out his hand to the lady. Her smile brightened just as quickly as if the sun came out from behind the clouds to shine just for him. Her glass of champagne was put down so quickly, the remains splashed against the rim before she placed her hand in his.

Without hesitation, he placed her trembling limb into the crook of his elbow and led her toward the ball-room. They had no need for words. The chords of a waltz struck up, and he whirled her into the pattern of the dance. She faltered only once before he tightened his hold upon her waist to steady her as other couples took to the floor.

"Are you enjoying your party, Lady Celia?" he asked, because that was the only thing he could think to say while holding her in his arms.

"It is amazing how I am enjoying it—far more than I was when I first arrived," she said.

A part of him was pleased at the implication. Was he the reason why her birthday was more pleasurable? "I suppose you will be attending the Season come the spring. I can only imagine your dance card will be filled every night once you have been received by the *ton*."

Her brow creased. "I had not thought of the coming Season, but yes, I suppose I will be in London by then."

Silence once more surrounded them, and they took two more turns around the ballroom before she spoke yet again. Something trivial, or was it?

"You dance divinely, my lord," she whispered, while she squeezed the hand that held her own.

"As do you, my lady." He smiled down into her face and noticed how slight she appeared in his arms. A reminder of how young she truly was.

Celia gave a breathy sigh. "I like the sound of that."

Adrian was puzzled trying to figure out what she was talking about. "The sound of what?" he asked.

She gave a light laugh. "The way you said *my* lady."

Now it was Adrian's turn to stumble. "It was only meant as a courtesy, Lady Celia. I can hardly claim you as *mine*." His reply caused her face to fall once more, and he cursed silently, knowing he was the reason.

She bit her lower lip in concentration before she raised her eyes to his expectantly. "You would only need to have a few words with my father to change the situation."

"I was under the impression that the duke favors Wyndham as your suitor."

"What if he does?" she retorted, harshly.

"I can hardly go against the wishes of your father if he desires you to wed Wyndham."

"I do not love Phillip."

"That will hardly matter if the duke already approves of the match," he replied, sharply.

Her brow rose. "You do not believe two people should love one another if they are to marry?" she asked with wide eyes.

"I never said love was not important between two people," he replied, even while he wondered how this conversation had taken a turn for the worse.

"Love is the most important part of being married."

He spun her around and continued the dance for several more steps before finally replying. "Not everyone has the luxury of actually loving the person they are to wed, let alone having their marriage based on love."

A gasp escaped her as though she could barely stand hearing such an admission. "What about what happened between us outside?" she asked in a hushed tone.

"What of it?" He cringed, hearing the words leak past his lips. Even to his own ears, they sounded callous and not what he intended.

Tears pooled in her eyes. "Do you care nothing for me?"

Adrian's gaze caught a look from the duke, who stood with the rest of the spectators watching the dancers. He was scowling, and the look was far from pleasant.

Adrian cleared his throat. "I never said I did not care for you, Celia."

"But you do not care enough to plead your cause to my father?"

"I did not say that either." He could see her temper rising, and Adrian was not sure he had ever seen this side of the young woman he held in his arms.

"Then what exactly *is* this between us, Adrian?"

He gave a heavy sigh. "I have no idea, my dear," he answered truthfully, because in all honesty he had no clue what had come over him since he met Celia at Hollystone Hall.

"Then I suggest, my lord, you figure it out, and quickly, before you are no longer left with any choice on the matter," Celia fumed.

The dance ended far too abruptly for Adrian's mental wellbeing. He bowed. Celia curtseyed and then stormed off the dance floor, leaving him wondering what the hell just happened.

He had no further time to ponder the lady and how much he had offended her, because the duke asked him to join him in Nicholas's study. The set down Adrian received for the next half hour made him feel as though he was still in the schoolroom being disciplined by an angry parent for failing at his lessons. The duke made his intentions perfectly clear where Celia was concerned, and Adrian had no choice but to agree to stay clear of his daughter.

As he left Nicholas's study, he caught a glimpse of the lady who had been stealing a piece of his heart without him even knowing it. She was lost to him, for he refused to go against her father's wishes and cause animosity within the family.

Adrian asked for his carriage to be brought around and, after a quick good-bye to his sister, left for his own estate. He swore he could still feel the taste of Celia's lips on his own far into the early morning hours. And when sleep finally overtook him, he dreamed of her naked in his arms, calling out his name...

CHAPTER 9

An estate outside of Bath
One Year Later
September, 1814

Celia stood with her sisters in an overly crowded room. Another house party, another ball, another round of invitations stretched before her, all rolling into the next until Celia felt she would go mad from it all. She had thought retiring to the country at the end of the Season would have won her some peace, but Father insisted on them moving from one social gathering to another.

She should have been enjoying herself, considering she had officially been launched into Society. But the more the weeks passed, the fouler her mood became. The only constant had been the marquis, whom she tolerated because her father insisted. She could hardly refuse his demands. *I am an obedient daughter* had become some kind of a chorus inside her head that helped her through yet another event.

She watched her father laughing across the room, a rare occurrence if there ever was one. Celia thought that with the birth of his heir, her father would have softened his demeanor toward his daughters. But nothing had changed, other than the duke doting upon his son. Christopher, or Kit as he had been nicknamed, was an adorable baby, and everyone was pleased with the latest edition to the family. The birth had taken its toll on her mother, however, and it was doubtful she would have any more children now that Kit was born.

Phillip nodded to her from across the room, and she returned the gesture. Was Celia being unfair to the marquis? He had done nothing to warrant her animosity toward him and had always been kind, if not overly so. Celia supposed she did not have any feelings for the man, mainly because she felt as though Phillip was being pushed upon her by her father as the only man worthy of marrying her. Maybe, at this point, not caring for Phillip was some instinctive ploy of hers to annoy her sire.

If she were honest with herself, there really was nothing wrong with Phillip. He was handsome enough, with his blond hair and striking grey eyes. Only five years separated them, so he still had that boyish, rakish charm that most ladies her own age loved. But Celia surmised it was Phillip's title and the fact that he, too, would be a duke one day that made all the difference to her father. In his eyes, Phillip was a more than suitable prize for his youngest daughter. Why her father was not pushing the marquis in either Elinor's or Alice's direction was beyond Celia. She only knew the duke sung Phillip's attributes constantly.

Celia continued her observation of the man her father had all but chosen for her to wed. Phillip had been courteous to a fault. A gentleman at all times. Maybe that was part of the problem. Maybe if he kissed her with the same amount of passion she had experienced with her very first kiss, she would no longer have the image of Adrian in her mind... and her heart.

She lifted her chin in defiance as Adrian crossed the room with Lady Sarah once again attached to his arm. How could he forget her so easily after what they had shared on her birthday? Maybe Adrian was right... love played no part in a marriage. If Phillip should offer for her, maybe she should just accept his proposal and give up all thoughts of love. Apparently, it was a foolish notion.

Brief bits of memory flashed through her mind while she remembered her last private conversation with Adrian nearly a year ago on her birthday. His kisses had stolen her breath away and still lingered in her head as if it were only yesterday she had been so happy to be in his arms. Even at family gatherings, he kept his distance, even going so far as to bring Lady Sarah with him to a Christmas dinner and to her brother's christening. The woman seemed to be his constant companion. Celia's heart had silently screamed at the unfairness of it all, but she could hardly complain, given her own escort was always near. God forbid if Adrian announced his plans to wed that woman. Celia knew her heart would never mend if Adrian married.

Celia watched Miranda saunter up to Phillip and link her arm through his. The two began whispering to one another, but it was the narrowing of Phillip's eyes that caused Celia to be concerned. What had Miranda said to the marquis to cause such a reaction? He began crossing the room, apparently heading in her direction. He did not look pleased.

A dreamy sigh distracted Celia from her thoughts.

"Is he not just the stuff dreams are made of?" Alice murmured, with a serene look upon her features.

Celia continued to watch Phillip's approach while a mask of politeness transformed his previously angry expression. "Yes, I suppose he is," she replied, trying to resign herself to her fate and her father's edict.

Alice's laughter rang out. "You are not even looking in the right direction, Celia," she exclaimed, amused.

Celia's brow creased in concentration as she tried to guess whom her sister might be speaking of. Certainly, enough handsome men thronged the room who might earn such a comment. "Who, exactly are you taking about?" she asked, ignoring Phillip when he was distracted by another guest who paused to speak with him.

Alice took Celia's arm, turning her slightly. "The Earl of Wayford, that is who," she said. "I swear I could melt in his arms and be perfectly content to remain there."

Celia's eyes widened as she looked upon the gentleman. Tall, with black hair, the Earl was certainly swoonworthy, with his dark complexion giving him a Mediterranean look leaning on the side of exotic. Greek or maybe Italian? Celia was uncertain about his nationality, since she had not been formally introduced to the man as yet. She could understand why Alice thought him handsome. He turned, and Celia held back a gasp when she viewed the multiple scars distorting his left cheek.

Elinor moved closer. "He has a horrible reputation, Alice—"

"Oh, who cares about his reputation," Alice said with a wave of her hand, as if such a matter could be so easily dismissed.

"—and is hardly marriage material," Elinor finished in a frantic whisper. "Why it is rumored his scars are from multiple duels fighting over women—with their husbands."

Celia snapped her fan open. "Father would never approve."

Elinor nodded. "No, he would not. Nor would he approve of us gossiping about one of the *ton*. I hate the thought of being put into the same category as the Danver sisters who spout every bit of tittle tattle they hear to that horrible editor at the *Teatime Tattler*."

"The Earl's mother, Lady Wayford, also tends to be at the root of every bit of gossip to hit Society on a daily basis," Celia added.

Alice was not deterred by their opinions as she rushed on. "I hear Lady Wayford is anxious for him to wed. I must find someone who can introduce us."

While Alice followed the Earl into the next room, where card tables had been set up, Celia noticed Miranda talking to another gentleman. The lady did not appear pleased.

Celia put her arm through Elinor's to get her attention. "Elinor, is that not the Marquis of Aldridge speaking with Miss de Courtenay?"

Elinor gasped. "Good heavens! I must find Lord de Courtenay since Grace is indisposed today." Celia saw her sister scan the room even while Adrian came up from behind the pair.

Her heart lurched again at the sight of him. Why did her feelings continue to betray her so? She had no further time to contemplate why she felt affection for a man who clearly did not care about her, for Phillip had joined her and offered his arm.

"Shall we take a stroll, my dear," he said. The cool tone to his normal jovial demeanor confused her. "I am told the gardens are still particularly lovely for this time of year."

"Yes, of course, my lord," Celia replied when she took his arm. "Please excuse us, Elinor."

Phillip took his time while he escorted her outside

to stroll among the blooming flowers. They continued their walk in silence, nodding to other couples who were also enjoying the garden paths. Phillip appeared to have a particular location in mind while he led her toward a towering hedge that must have been well over six feet tall. A maze? He certainly did not think to take her inside a maze without a chaperone present, or did he?

Celia's steps faltered at the entrance. "My lord, I cannot accompany you inside a maze," she said, her heart beating furiously at the thought of being caught alone with him.

"There is no reason to think we shall be alone, my dear," he said with a wink. "There are plenty of others inside, and I understand this one is easy to figure out, so you may quickly find your way back outside."

As if to prove his point, two laughing couples emerged from the maze. "I suppose it will be permissable," she finally answered.

She took his arm again as he whisked her inside. Immediately, she became hopelessly lost after he had made only a few twists and turns as though he knew this maze from past experience. His declaration that other people would be inside must have been pure conjecture on his part, for they did not meet another living creature except a few birds chirping to one another at the top of the greenery.

They reached the center. A granite statue of a woman rose majestically from a fountain surrounded by a few benches. Before Celia could ask Phillip to return her to the party, he pushed her up against the hedge causing the stems to scratch her bare skin. She turned her head and felt a trickle of blood run down her cheek.

His breath was hot on her neck. "I have waited months to taste you. Give me a sample of what I hear you gave to de Courtenay. Make me forget you have been with another man and are not the virgin you pretend to be."

His husky words were strained. Before Celia could refute his words, his mouth swooped down to claim her own in a demanding, possessive kiss. It took all her energy to hold the man off from doing anything more than kiss her. She needed help, and it appeared as though no one would be coming to her aid!

CHAPTER 10

Adrian began making his way in the direction of his sister Miranda who was standing with the Marquis of Aldridge. Grace had told Adrian what had happened between their sister and the marquis and his brother. Adrian could never condone the methods they used to teach Miranda a well-deserved lesson. Certainly, she should not have been pursuing Aldridge just to win a meaningless bet with Grace that the marquis would propose marriage.

But Adrian would do all in his power to protect his youngest sister, whatever her faults. She could have been hurt—would have, had anyone overheard the two men comment on her forwardness and propose to share her as their mistress. She appeared no better pleased with the current conversation. Adrian paused before he reached them to overhear what they were saying. His forehead furrowed at their words.

"Miss de Courtenay, you tread on thin ice when you play with the hearts of others." Aldridge's bored mien did not change, but his tone was censorious.

One delicate brow rose as Miranda peeked up at him through her lashes. "I have no idea what you are talking about."

He stepped closer. "I had hoped you learned your lesson at Hollystone, but I fear I was mistaken."

"How dare you bring up the horrible situation you and Lord Jonathan put me in," she fumed. "I no longer make silly bets with Grace—"

Aldridge frowned. "—and yet you continue to play games with the emotions of others. I thought you and Lady Celia were friends."

"We are." Her fan flipped open to cool her suddenly flushed face.

It was Aldridge's turn to raise his brow. "Then why converse with Wyndham as if you have taken him as your lover?"

She slapped the fan shut. "How dare you!"

He gave a small chuckle, devoid of amusement. "No daring required. I overheard your talk with the marquis. It is clear to everyone except Lady Celia that you want him for yourself."

Adrian had heard enough and stepped forward.

"Adrian!" Miranda's voiced carried farther than necessary, and several people turned in their direction. "Whatever are you doing here?"

Adrian bowed to Aldridge. "My lord, will you excuse us so I might have a private word with my sister?"

Aldridge returned the bow to Adrian. "Of course." His nod to Miranda was a shade less than a bow. "Miss de Courtenay."

Adrian took his sister's elbow, and they moved to a secluded alcove. "What the devil are you doing with Aldridge?"

"Nothing at all," she replied with a toss of her head, "idle chit chat. Nothing more."

"What I overheard did not sound like a mere chance to catch up or talk about the weather."

"I am telling you, we had a meaningless conversation. I am certain Aldridge has already forgotten I am even present."

"Then please explain what you have done to Lady Celia and why Wyndham appeared distressed as he led her from the room. What did you say to him?" Adrian growled out.

Miranda peeked at him before a sly smile crept up at the corner of her mouth. "Well... I may have mentioned that you and Celia had a little encounter on the balcony at her birthday last fall," she said before she flipped her fan open again.

"How the hell did *you* come by such information?"

She tapped him on the arm with her fan. "She confided in me one night when she was crying her eyes out that you would no longer speak to her. Really, Adrian, you are such a cad. Do you not know you broke that poor girl's heart? You kiss her senseless one night, then do not give her a second thought afterwards."

Adrian rubbed at his neck in frustration. He had thought of Celia for months but refused to go against her father's wishes. He had not been selfish enough to tell Celia, not wanting her at odds with her father. "It is none of your business what happened between Celia and myself."

"Well, someone needed to console her, and she is my friend," she said, then got a far off look. "Lord Wyndham appeared upset at the information you had kissed her."

"If she is your friend, why would you reveal such a private matter?" he hissed.

Miranda shrugged her shoulders. "Maybe you should go check on them. I may have made a mistake telling Phillip."

"Do you *think* so?" he muttered, but continuing on without allowing her to answer. "Where did they go?"

Miranda waved her hand in the air. "The gardens, I think, or maybe the maze. I was not paying much attention after the marquis swore in front of me. Can you imagine it? A gentleman swearing in front of a lady!"

The maze? That had disaster written all over it. Adrian warned his sister to behave herself. He should have been concerned when she laughed and then left him standing there as though she had not a care in the world.

Adrian hurried out of the veranda doors to look for

Lady Celia, hoping she was not in danger from Wyndham. He lengthened his stride, having a feeling in the pit of his belly she was in need of his aid.

⚜

Celia struggled against Phillip; his hands moved with alarming speed up her body. Had he, of a sudden, grown a second pair of limbs? His mouth continued his torturous assault on hers, but when one of his fingers plunged into the neckline of her bodice, a scream of outrage tore from her throat.

She managed to squeeze her hands between them and press firmly against his solid chest. It was enough to break contact with his lips. "Get. Off. Me!" she fumed. With all her strength, she gave him a mighty shove. The sound of tearing fabric seemed to break whatever had possessed Phillip as he stumbled backwards.

"Celia..." he began, even while his eyes devoured what the rip displayed for his viewing pleasure.

She looked down. Gasping, she tugged at her chemise and vainly attempted to pull together what she could of her gown. She turned from his view, embarrassed not only by the fact her breasts had been exposed, but also that he had put her in such a position.

Tears filled her eyes. "How could you?" she finally managed to whisper.

"I apologize for my actions, Celia. I only know that when I heard you had been with de Courtenay, a jealousy I have never known before overcame me." His eyes seemed to plead with her to understand.

She would have none of what he tried to offer as an explanation. "You should not listen to idle gossip, my lord," she hissed.

"I swear upon my honor the information was from a reliable source."

A laugh escaped her bruised lips. "Honor? You have no honor, Phillip, or is there some part of this situation that is escaping me?" He took a step closer, and she thrust one hand forward to halt his progress. "Do not *dare* come near me!"

"You must forgive me," he begged, a worried frown creased his brow.

He appeared sincere, but how could Celia trust him when but moments ago he was ready to take her here... in the garden maze... for anyone to come upon them to witness her disgrace?

"Forgive you?" she snapped. "Forgive you for trying to dishonor me or for listening to the gossiping of others? Which offense should we address first, Phillip?"

"Surely you must know I wish you to become my bride." His casual tone and stance irritated her further.

"And just because you and my father desire our union, you feel that this..." Celia waved her hand back and forth in the air, "gives you permission to assault me like a common trollop?"

Phillip looked down to examine his signet ring as

though he were bored. "Given what I was told, I felt I was within my rights, considering we are to marry."

"I have never consented to become your wife," she fumed, her face flushing in anger.

"Yes, well, that was the plan, but I must admit I have no desire to take the leavings of another. I will need proof that you remain a virgin before I formally offer for you. I am certain you understand that a man in my position cannot possibly take a soiled bride to wife."

Celia's mouth opened and closed several times while trying to form some kind of a response. Clutching the fabric of her torn dress, she stepped forward. "I will never marry you after this, Phillip."

The marquis looked her up and down. She clenched her fists while awaiting his reply, ready to further stand her ground. "The situation will need to be discussed with your father." His reply, as though nothing had changed between them, caught her off guard, even as he continued on. "That is... if I still wish to wed you."

The nerve of this arrogant buffoon, she thought. Outraged that he still thought she might consider him for a husband burst forth. "You are not the man I would ever want to marry. Now get out of my sight!"

Phillip had the decency to keep his thoughts to himself and finally left her to walk back into the maze. Celia swiped away tears of frustration before her situation caught up with her and her sobs turned to true grief.

What had Phillip been told for him to act in such an

ungentlemanly manner, and who would say such things about her? The harder she thought of the rumors that must be floating around the *ton* about her, the harder she began to cry. And her father... if her father found out what had just happened, would he put the blame on her or where it truly belonged?

Celia peered down at her torn bodice and the scratches on her arms. Her hands flew to her face wondering what other damage had been done as panic overtook her.

How would she leave the maze looking like this? And with half of Society visiting the manor, she would be hard pressed to remain unseen. New tears fell, and she covered her face with her hands to once more sob out her anguish.

"What the devil did Wyndham do to you?"

Oh, God, not him! Her heart raced while she prayed for strength to pull herself together. But as she raised her eyes and saw Adrian's angry expression, her resolution to remain strong quickly vanished. He was her weakness. The one man who had crushed her spirits and did not even realize he had done such a dastardly deed.

Fresh tears streaked down her cheeks. They were caused not by what she had endured from Phillip but by a broken heart that would not heal.

"Oh, Adrian..." His name, torn from her lips, was a heartfelt plea, a last vain entreaty for him to love her. Still... her tone alone conveyed everything she could have possibly said, especially given her situation. The past and present began converging upon her emotions... emotions that could no longer be held back.

And as Adrian folded her into his embrace, Celia's tears fell even harder than before. Once he learned what Philip had done to her, there would be no chance Adrian would ever love her. She was soiled and Celia knew in her heart this would be the last time she would ever be held in his arms again.

CHAPTER 11

Adrian could stand anything but her tears...

When Celia's tear streaked face rose to stare upon him, all he could see was her eyes beseeching him to understand. Yet only she knew for sure what she had been through with Wyndham. He folded her into his arms before he even realized he had done so, whispering words of comfort in some attempt to take away the hurt caused by another.

"You are safe, my lady, and I vow to always protect you," he murmured, caressing her hair while her head rested upon his shoulder. How could he have forgotten how right it felt to hold her, to have her within his embrace? He kissed the top of her head trying to think of some way to turn their situation around so he might have her father's approval.

"You vow to always protect me?" she sighed as

though her dreams of him being with her would be coming to fruition.

"Yes, well, as I should, considering you are family."

"You make such a vow too lightly, my lord. You are hardly in a position to offer your protection," she snapped while pushing upon his chest. Instead of letting her go, he held her tighter.

Adrian swore he heard her mutter a curse. Unprepared when she ripped herself from his arms, his brows narrowed when he took a good look at her condition as she began gathering the remnants of her torn dress together.

"I will kill him for touching you!"

"And cause a scandal? I highly doubt you would dare make such a scene, especially since you made it perfectly clear by the lack of your presence that you do not care one fig about what becomes of me," she sneered. Disdain dripped from her words and cut straight to his heart.

He now understood how much he had hurt her with his absence. For months, he had been telling himself he stayed away to honor her father's wishes. He had never intended to break her heart, but he could see for himself that he had.

Adrian held out his hand for her to take, but Celia ignored him while making a further attempt to cover herself. "I never said I did not care for you," he finally answered after a heavy sigh.

"You never *said* anything at all!" Celia's voice echoed

off into the air, causing several birds to take flight. Her tone testified how angry she was with him, and he could not blame her.

"You do not understand—" he began.

Celia stood in front of him and poked him in his chest.

"—nor do I have to listen to your half empty attempt at an apology," she finished. "I am afraid such a chance passed you by months ago."

"There is a reason—"

"—And I no longer care to listen to you spout some meaningless explanation in order for you to vindicate your sense of honor," she fumed.

"Celia, please listen to me," Adrian tried again but clamped his lips shut when she held up her hand and raised her chin in a semblance of defiance.

"You obviously have no feelings for me and have no plans to offer a marriage between us. It may have taken me a full year to come to terms with your rejection, but I certainly do not need you hovering over me proposing whatever protection you may feel I need. I can take care of myself."

His mouth formed into a line of displeasure while his eyes skimmed over her torn bodice. "Yes... I can certainly see what a good job you are doing taking care of yourself, my dear."

Crack! His head snapped sideways from the impact; his cheek felt as if it were on fire. *Well deserved.* He should never have implied she could not take care of herself. He should never have reminded her of what almost happened, of how she appeared. She was embarrassed enough without him causing further insult.

Fresh tears flowed down her cheeks. "Stay away from me, Adrian de Courtenay." She tore the necklace he had given her for her birthday from her neck and flung it on the ground.

Another sob was ripped from her throat, and he hated knowing he was now the cause. She ran from him, turning into the maze. "Celia, I am sorry," he shouted before he picked up her discarded jewelry and followed. He refused to allow their relationship to end on such a sour note. If nothing else, they would be thrown together at every family gathering for the rest of their lives.

"Celia," he called out. He stopped to listen, desperate to find her. The sound of crying reached his ears. He raced in her direction, only to meet a wall of hedge. Damn maze!

"Celia!"

"Go away, Adrian," she called out in the distance.

Turning around, he went in the opposite direction, and after several misguided turns, Adrian finally caught a glimpse of her dress as she rounded a corner ahead of him. He lengthened his stride, quickly catching up to her just before she left the maze. Adrian took hold of her arm, swinging her around, but she struggled against him as if he was her mortal enemy.

"Stay away from me," she said, tugging at her arm.

He attempted to pull her closer. "If you would just listen to me, Celia. I never—"

"Let go of me, you cur. Never touch me again. Have you not done enough damage to me already?"

He tugged, she pulled, and before he could respond to her outburst, they lost their footing. Falling forward towards the entrance to the maze, Adrian wound his arms around Celia's waist and rolled to prevent her from landing upon the ground. They fell chest to chest with her on top. Their eyes locked and held one to the other in another moment that seemed frozen in time. With their breathing ragged and chests heaving, Adrian realized he could feel every luscious curve of her body. He certainly did not wish to let her go... at least not with her angry with him.

"Celia..." her name was like a soft caress when it escaped his lips. Before he could offer an apology, the world as he knew it split completely apart.

"Oh, my!" a woman's voice exclaimed, startled. "This is highly inappropriate."

"Your Grace... I had no idea we would find my brother with your daughter like this," Miranda said. Her overly sweet tone churned Adrian's stomach.

He saw Celia's eyes widen into startled surprise then turn to a mix of embarrassment and fear, as was inevitable given they had fallen into what appeared to be an embrace. Their heads turned simultaneously to stare alarmed at the spectacle before them beyond the entrance to the maze.

"Oh, no," Celia whispered.

"Oh, yes," Adrian grimly replied.

Celia began fumbling to stand, but her dress seemed to have a mind of its own while the fabric tangled itself around his legs. With the damn muslin freed, they were able to at last get to their feet. Adrian placed Celia behind him, not wishing her to be seen. Apparently, half the *ton* had decided a walk in the garden was just what they needed to complete their day.

CHAPTER 12

Although Celia was still spitting mad at Adrian, she welcomed him intervening to hide her current condition from all of Society. She stole a peek around the protective barrier he offered and instantly regretted it.

Her father's face was flushed an unsightly shade of purple. His mouth moved as if to say something before his lips snapped shut. Behind him, Lady Wayford looked completely aghast and was already whispering to the other matronly ladies next to her. They quickly took their leave. Miranda was clinging once more to Phillip, who looked outraged as though he had not been the reason her gown was in complete tatters. Silence filled the garden area. A crowd gazed with open curiosity at them, and Celia could only imagine what was going through their minds.

Miranda took a step forward. Something flashed

briefly in her eyes before they appeared etched in concern. "Celia, dear... you should have been more specific and careful when you asked me to find your father because you wished to show him something in the gardens. If I had known you were having a secret meeting with my brother, why... I would have delayed bringing him outside for a while longer."

"What? I never—"

Adrian whirled around so fast Celia took several steps backwards. How their situation had suddenly changed, for now it was his turn to be furious... with her!

"You and my sister planned this?" he roared.

"I did no such thing," Celia retaliated.

"It is certainly convenient, then, that in the eyes of everyone present, you are ruined, and I am the culprit," he growled out, before waving his hand in the direction of the crowd that appeared to be growing by the second.

"I am telling you; I planned nothing," Celia argued. Did he truly know so little about her that he could think she would risk her reputation to such a scheme? She had never been one to play games with the emotions of others.

"If you were looking to snatch a husband, then I applaud you, my lady, for your plan has succeeded."

Her breath left her when his icy gaze landed upon her with all the contempt he was obviously feeling. Those close enough to hear his words began to laugh, and Celia swayed, praying to God she would not faint. "I never planned this, Adrian," she repeated. "You will have to discuss this fiasco with your sister, for I have not been privy to this *supposed* conversation between us."

They both turned their attention momentarily to Miranda, who had the decency to drop her eyes to examine the ground before he continued. "You should have stuck to your original choice of the marquis for a husband. Holding out to become a duchess one day would have been a far loftier goal. Now, you will have to settle for being a mere countess." Adrian's words were strained when they passed his lips, his fists curled at his sides.

But it was the furious glint in his eyes that broke Celia's heart all over again. It was one thing to know she would never have his love, but to see his scorching sneer, as though he loathed the very sight of her, was more than she could bear.

She searched his face for some flicker of understanding, but she saw nothing in his features to show he would believe her, let alone ever trust her again.

"Please understand..." she choked out, unable to endure the silence that had fallen between them.

"Elinor!" Celia winced at the sound of her father's angry voice ringing out so loud that those inside the manor could have heard him. "Your sister is in need of your assistance. Lend her your wrap and make your way to our carriage. We will be leaving shortly. Lord de Courtenay..."

Her father's words trailed off. There was no way to mistake their meaning or his direct order for a private conversation between them. Celia stepped forward to take hold of the edges of Adrian's jacket. "Please listen to me, Adrian," she begged in a soft murmur.

He roughly pulled her hands from his garment and pushed her away as though her touch was an offense against his person. "As you would not give me a moment to hear my plea, I will extend you the same courtesy. Now... if you will excuse me, I believe your father and I must speak on a matter of grave importance."

His obligatory bow was unnaturally stiff, and Celia watched him leave with her father. Elinor wrapped a shawl around her shoulders and an arm around her waist for support as they left the garden.

As they made their way through the manor, Celia could already hear the sniggering of the *ton*. She was ruined. Disgraced. Dishonored in the eyes of all those who were present. She somehow managed to hold her head high, but all efforts to keep her dignity fled the moment the carriage door shut the rest of the world out from her view. Celia slid across the seat to take her place in one of the corners. Nothing could stop her hands from trembling along with the rest of her body. What was to become of her now?

A short while later, Adrian handed Miranda into their carriage then rapped on the roof. With the crack of the leather reins and a lurch of their conveyance, they were on their way back to his country estate. It took every bit of whatever self-control he still possessed not to throttle his sister. What the devil had she been thinking?

The brief meeting with the duke was far shorter than Adrian had expected. More cordial, too, except at the beginning. His Grace began their impromptu meeting by demanding satisfaction for ruining his daughter before he realized he could not challenge Adrian to a duel. Instead, Adrian stood completely still as the duke's fist slammed into his face. He supposed a black eye was more than enough compensation for the insult caused to His Grace's family name and was preferable to a bullet.

Once His Grace composed himself again, the result of their meeting was more of a formality. Brief. Direct. Certainly, there was no question that Adrian would agree to marry the duke's daughter in order to right the wrong done this day. There was no point trying to persuade His Grace that Adrian was not the one to have caused his daughter's initial condition and torment. Wyndham was not the one who had been caught in such a compromising situation. Adrian's whole life had been turned upside down by two scheming women!

Under normal circumstances, Adrian would have been thrilled to have the man's consent to wed Celia.

But starting a marriage with a lie after being duped into their arrangement was a far cry from the wedded bliss Adrian had dreamed of when he finally took a woman to wife.

He tore his gaze from the passing scenery to peer at his sister in the seat across from him. She looked calm, as though nothing untoward had occurred when nothing could be further from the truth. His life would never be the same now that he was being coerced into marriage. But what to do with his mischievous sister was beyond him. It was one thing to have a silly bet between sisters go astray and entirely another when such a prank affected others.

"I know not what you sought to gain by such a display, but I hope you are satisfied with the results, dear Miranda," he said, trying to figure out what game she now played.

Miranda continued to watch the scenery through the window and even had the gall to wave to a couple as they passed by.

"At least have the decency to look at me," he growled out, his anger rising at her lack of a response.

She took a moment to untie the ribbons of her bonnet and place it on the seat next to her before turning her attention to him. "What did you wish to speak about?"

"You can honestly ask such an insane question?"

Miranda shrugged her shoulders. "I did nothing you will not thank me for one day."

"Well, I am not thanking you today! You meddle in the lives of others as if we were but pawns on a chess board." He ran his hand across the nape of his neck, frustrated that a sister of his cared only for herself.

"I hardly think of this as a game, Adrian," she murmured. For an instant, he could see regret pass across her features before her mask of triviality fell back into place.

"At least we are in agreement on that account. What have I ever done to you that you and Lady Celia would stoop so low as to enact this unkind trick to ensure we would be forced to marry?"

Miranda remained silent, her fingers silently tapping the edge of the seat. She turned to look out the window once more, her fan flipping open to fan her face.

Adrian had had enough. "Answer me, Miranda!"

Her fan snapped shut before she pointed it at him like some kind of a weapon. Her face flushed in anger. "You and Gracie were always jealous of me being the favorite of mama and papa. With them passing from this earth, neither of you care one bit about me. You leave it to me to make sure I have a titled husband to call my own," she shouted, before she clamped her lips shut. Tears began running down her cheeks.

Adrian sat there, stunned at her outburst before her words struck a chord. "Wyndham? You thought he would be a wise choice in a husband?"

"Celia made it clear she did not want him. Why

should I not do everything in my power to see about one day becoming his duchess?"

Adrian sat forward to peer at his sister. "And you and Celia thought that by forcing a scene, this would pave the way to you having Wyndham?"

She refused to meet his eyes, turning her head towards the window again before she answered him. "It seemed a logical solution to both our problems."

Adrian frowned. Celia had insisted that she had known nothing, but Miranda had claimed they had planned this together. Could Miranda be lying? "Tell me the truth, Miranda. Did Celia know about this plot."

Miranda gave a short laugh but still would not look at him. "What? Do you think I chose to do this on my own? Of course, Celia and I discussed it." She slid a glance at him, then looked down at her hands, which were twisting the ribbons of her bonnet. "I will admit that it was my idea."

Adrian heaved a heavy sigh. "You should have learned a lesson with that whole business at Hollystone, but I can see now that the mistake was made when I did not take a firmer hand in making sure you behaved in a manner befitting your station."

"What station?" she demanded. "I have no title and am nothing but a common *Miss*."

"There is nothing *common* about you, Miranda, except the thoughts inside your pretty little head. You have meddled in the lives of others for the last time."

Her eyes widened. "What is *that* supposed to mean?" she asked in a frantic whisper.

"Only that I am washing my hands of you. With the season already over, everyone is retiring to the countryside. No one will think it overly strange if we retire there as well. I will write to Grace and see if she will take you in. Hopefully, with the new baby, you will not be too much of a burden on their household."

"But I do not want to live with Grace and Nicholas. Why, they barely leave Highgrove Manor anymore. You would exile me with them and their baby so I cannot attend any social functions at all?"

"There shall be no better place for you to contemplate your actions and to keep you from causing further trouble in the lives of others. Maybe this time you shall learn your lesson... at least one can hope."

She began to pout as though this might change his mind. "You hate me."

He looked upon his sister almost as if seeing her for the first time. "Hate you? No... I do not hate you, Miranda. You are my family, and I love you dearly." He noticed the gleam of satisfaction that sparked for a moment in her eyes. His narrowed, and he hesitated only a moment before he continued. "What I *hate* is your manipulation of situations that you think will gain you what you desire, careless of the harm to others. And *that*, my dear, ends here and now."

The fleeting thought that she would get her way quickly passed, leaving her crestfallen. Or was this just another ploy on her part? It was difficult to tell with Miranda.

The rest of their ride was silent, and the carriage began to slow as they neared his country manor. Strange, how the house looked unchanged when his mind was raging at the position he had been placed in. He took out his watch fob and noted the time, while coming to a decision he should have taken care of months ago.

Miranda grabbed her bonnet. "Let us discuss this further in your study, Adrian," she all but demanded. The footman opened the door while Adrian remained seated.

"I have another pressing engagement," he replied dryly.

"At this hour?" she asked, alighting from the carriage before swinging back around to peer inside at him. "Please, Adrian. Send the driver to the stables with the carriage and come inside."

"I am afraid I must decline," he said, not looking forward to his next confrontation.

She narrowed her eyes, but he would not be swayed. "Whatever am I to do with my evening... alone... again?" she cried out.

"Perhaps you should think about packing, my dear. After all, thanks to you, the family will soon be preparing for a wedding."

Before she could reply, he nodded to the footman, who closed the door while Miranda hastily ran up the steps and went inside the manor. He rapped on the roof. His driver slid open a compartment, and Adrian told him to head to London. He needed to let Josephine go, and he prayed he would not be subjected to another woman's tears. He was not sure how much more he could stand in one day.

After spending the night at an inn, Adrian arrived at his London town house by mid-afternoon. He put off the inevitable confrontation for several more hours by first taking care of business matters that needed his attention. He finally called for his carriage, and twenty minutes later, he was entering Josephine's foyer and handing his hat to her butler. In the front parlor, he helped himself to a snifter of brandy before turning to stare out the window. Swirling the amber liquid around in the glass, he took several sips before he heard Josephine coming into the room.

"Adrian, darling... I am so happy to see you."

He swivelled upon his heels to see her welcoming smile. "Hello, Josephine." His face must have told her much, for he watched her happy expression fade to one of concern.

"Is something the matter?" she asked, coming forward and taking his hand to lead him over to a comfortable settee.

He gulped down the last of the brandy, and she took the empty snifter before moving closer. Her hands clutched at his, almost as if she knew their association was about to end. "I came to say good-bye."

She winced at his words. "But you just arrived." Hope rang in her voice. He hated to disappoint her.

"You should congratulate me, my dear. You see before you a man who is about to be married," his voice dripped with sarcasm, while her eyes widened in alarm.

"I see," she managed to finally murmur. "I had no idea you were officially seeing anyone."

"I was not. The *situation* was unplanned," he relied curtly, "but still necessary."

"Who is she?" she murmured.

"Does it matter?" he replied. The reason he and Celia were getting married was of no consequence. However, he refused to defame her good name by divulging such information to his mistress.

"No. I suppose it does not," Josephine said, her voice shaking with emotion.

She stood, distancing herself from him by crossing the room to go to the sideboard. Her hands clutched the edges, her knuckles turning white. She heaved a heavy sigh before reaching to pour herself a sherry. She took a drink before turning to face him again.

"It sounds as though you do not care for this future wife of yours," Josephine surmised. "If such is the case, I see no reason why we cannot continue our arrangement."

"I never said I did not care for her. I do not care for the reason we shall wed."

"She tricked you?" she asked before taking another

sip of her sherry. "Really, darling... How could you be so careless?"

"And foolish?" he added, watching her shrug.

"I would never dare call you foolish, Adrian." Setting the glass down, she came back over to him and sat in his lap. She began nuzzling his neck. "How long can you stay tonight?"

Adrian pulled her arms from around his neck. "I cannot stay and will not be back."

"I see," she whispered. "What will become of me?"

Tears welled within her eyes, and he could barely stand another woman being hurt on his account. Not today. Not after everything he had already been through. He helped her off his lap and had to admit it was a welcome relief. Having her so close to his body made him feel as if he betrayed Celia. He should not let such a thought bother him but somehow it did. *Bloody hell!*

Adrian stood and took Josephine's hand, bringing it to his lips. "I shall settle all your accounts and ensure you have a sizable amount deposited into your name at your bank. Use those funds however you wish, but know I cannot provide further for you. I am certain you shall have no trouble finding my replacement."

"No one could replace you, Adrian," she declared, her hushed tone barely above a whisper. "Are you certain you do not wish to continue as we have? I do not mind that you will be married."

He gave her a brief smile before she stood taking

both his hands again. "But I do. I could not, in all good conscious, carry on an affair when I will be married. I have a duty to her and my family."

Josephine pursed her lips, holding in her emotions. "You love her."

Adrian was surprised at how true her words rang. "Yes... I suppose I do," he finally admitted. "Although I cannot in all honestly easily forgive the woman for her part in the game she played."

He gave Josephine another smile even as she clung to his hands. He gave a slight tug until she at last let go.

"She is a very lucky woman... whoever she is. I envy her," Josephine whispered, while a single tear raced down her cheek.

He smirked before he traced away her tear with his thumb. "Do not be too envious of her, my dear Josephine. My soon-to-be bride will not be living in wedded bliss with our marriage anytime soon. In fact, she is about to learn about hell on earth."

"I wish you well, my lord," Josephine replied while her eyes appeared to be drinking in the sight of him.

"Goodbye, Josephine," he said. He supposed he held her face longer than he should have, considering he was ending their association. "Thank you for everything."

He kissed her cheek and retrieved his hat from her butler. With one more glance at the woman who had given him many hours of pleasure, he left, but was only half way down the walk before he heard something shattering inside. Some costly vase had met its demise.

His driver opened the door, but Adrian hesitated before he entered the carriage.

He looked back to find Josephine staring out of the window at him, her hand clutching at the collar of her robe. Tears freely fell from her eyes, and the sight was burned forever into his head. He had hurt her with his news. This was something he could not undo, and even though he had to leave her, he had appreciated the time spent with her.

He gave her one last nod, and she waved her hand in return. Stepping up into the carriage, he took his seat, and the horses were put into motion, taking him home.

Once there, he made his way to his room with a bottle of brandy. He was determined to dull the pain in his heart. But the reason behind his foul mood was not that he had given his ex-mistress his dismissal. No... it was all due to a woman he had fallen in love with. A woman he cared for but who had thoughtlessly duped him into their marriage... unless, of course, Miranda's words were a lie. But no. Surely she would not lie to his face, when her friend was the one who would bear the consequences. Either way, surely it would require a full bottle to dull the emotions he was feeling.

CHAPTER 13

November, 1814

Celia sat is a small room outside of the family chapel with only her sisters for company. Her mother was attending Kit. Her father, barely able to stand the sight of her since her downfall two months ago, was somewhere waiting for the groom to arrive. Adrian was late, and Celia was beginning to worry he would call off the whole thing. They had not spoken more than a dozen words since that fateful day that changed both their lives.

Memories assaulted her mind, especially the day when Adrian had come to call at her father's country estate near Bath to give her an engagement ring. It should have one of the happiest days of their lives as they celebrated their upcoming union. Instead, she was treated to cool civility and utter disdain. Gone were

Adrian's twinkling blue eyes when he called her his little bird or sparrow. Gone were his teasing remarks that caused her heart to flutter in her chest or her breath to leave her because he was bestowing her a small measure of affection.

With her parents present, he had bowed low, murmuring nonsense about the honor she did him before he placed a diamond ring of some worth upon her finger. Her own response was just as flat as his proposal. Just as swiftly, he had left, as quietly as he had come. She had not seen him since except at a distance at a few family functions.

The door opened, and Grace entered. Celia caught a brief glimpse of Miranda waiting in the antechamber with a worried expression before the door closed off the rest of the world. Her aunt came to her and took her hands.

"How beautiful you look, Celia," Grace murmured, bending down to give Celia a kiss upon her cheek. "Adrian will be overcome with joy once he sees you walking down the aisle."

Celia felt a small measure of hope rise inside her chest. "Do you think so?" Her voice quavered as she gave a quick prayer. For despite everything, she was still in love with the man. Once she had calmed down, she realized the truth of that. Sure, he acted in anger and hurt pride, but deep down, Celia knew he was still the same man she had fallen in love with oh so long ago.

Grace gave her hands a reassuring squeeze. "Of

course, he will, my dear. Why no bride has ever looked as lovely as you do at their wedding."

Celia laughed for the first time in days. "Every bride looks beautiful when they are about to be married, Aunt Grace. Besides, you have to say such wonderful things. You are the wife of my beloved uncle."

Grace kissed her forehead. "I only speak the truth."

"Has he arrived?" Celia asked, knowing she did not have to say Adrian's name. Everyone was concerned that the hour appointed for the ceremony was thirty minutes ago, and he had yet to arrive. If he did not show, there would be no chance of saving what remained of her reputation.

Grace blushed. "Not yet, but do not fear. I know my brother, and he will have a reasonable explanation as to his tardiness."

"I will have to take your word for it," Celia said, knowing she sounded as crestfallen as she no doubt felt.

Grace appeared worried when she spoke. "I am here on an entirely different matter."

"Is something wrong?" Celia asked nervously.

"I came on behalf of my sister. She wondered if you might give her a moment so she could apologize for—"

"No." Celia's answer was simple. She had not spoken to Miranda since she betrayed their friendship.

"But if you would only listen, Celia. She is family and—"

"—and she should have known better than to inter-fere and lie when such a falsehood affected the lives of others. I am sorry, Aunt Grace, but I am not in the mood to forgive her, especially not today of all days," Celia angrily replied. This whole situation was all Miranda's fault, and she would in no way ease the girl's conscience as yet.

Grace nodded. "Please forgive me for bringing up such a delicate matter, Celia. It was inconsiderate of me, but you cannot fault me for trying to mend the rift between two people I care so much about. Adrian will not listen to me, but I hoped perhaps..."

Celia gazed upon her aunt's distressed features. "You are not to blame for any of this, Grace, but I am sure you can also understand the reason behind my refusal."

The door opened again to admit Celia's mother, giving Grace no chance to reply. "He has arrived, Celia."

Elinor handed Celia her bouquet of flowers. "And he is long overdue," she replied with a frown. "A gentleman never keeps a lady waiting."

Celia took up the flowers. "Leave it be, Elinor."

Alice reached up to place Celia's veil over her face. "You cannot blame our sister for being upset with him," she said, taking up Elinor's defense. "We want you to be happy, Celia."

Celia sighed, staring at the flowers in her hand. "Shall we get this formality over with?"

She left the room, the women following in her wake. She waited before the doors while her mother, sisters, and Grace took their seats. The organ struck a chord, and her father stiffly offered his arm. She took it with a trembling hand. No words of encouragement. No loving words to a beloved daughter. Nothing. Why did she still expect something from this uncaring man?

Celia's steps faltered, but she quickly recovered. The church was relatively empty. Only family members and a few close friends were seated in the first few pews. This was certainly not how she had imagined her wedding.

As she continued her walk down the aisle, Adrian at last turned to meet her, and for one instant, she saw a flicker of his old self as his gaze fell appreciatively on her. Just as quickly, he masked his feelings from view. She thought she had accepted the reality of her situation, but his cold expression chilled her heart.

Her father took his place next to her mother. Celia took Adrian's arm as they knelt before the altar, and Celia gave up her childhood fantasy of wedded bliss to a loving husband.

The priest droned on about the importance of marriage, but Celia heard little of what the man was saying. Instead, she glanced sideways at her groom. She had never seen Adrian look more handsome, and the part of her that still loved him cried out for the injustice of starting their lives together with him hating her. She had done nothing wrong, yet he still refused to listen to reason.

When they stood to say their vows to one another, Adrian's voice rang out strong while her tone was barely above a whisper. With a few more words, a band of gold was slipped onto her finger. Adrian then pulled the silky veil from her face and placed a brief chaste kiss upon her lips to seal their union.

The doors to the church were opened for them as they left. There were no children outside throwing flower petals and certainly no villagers to toss coins to in celebration of their wedding. Only the cold wind of autumn greeted them, a grim reminder to Celia of what awaited her in this marriage. She should not expect anything from Adrian other than the contempt he bore her since Miranda had devised this whole ruse.

She drew up her courage as they walked along the stone path back to her parents' manor for their wedding dinner. "Will you not speak with me, Adrian?" she asked while she watched his features. Another flicker of surprise washed across his face. Was it only hope that hinted at a brief crack in the wall he had placed between them? If so, he covered it quickly.

"What would you like to speak of, Celia? Shall we talk about the weather or something more personal like the reason you betrayed me?"

"We could have cleared this whole nasty business rather quickly two months ago if you would have only listened to me," she replied quietly.

"The results would have been the same. We are wed. You got what you wanted and that was a ring on your finger. Unfortunately, your fellow conspirator will never have Wyndham. I refuse to let the man near my sister, especially knowing what he did before I came upon you."

"Miranda wished to marry Phillip?" she asked, aghast she had not seen the signs for herself.

He peered at her from his towering height. "If I did not know better, my dear, I would believe your little act that you knew nothing. But that is of no consequence now. I applaud your ingenuity even as I detest how far you would actually go to hook me into our current predicament. In the years to come, I hope you enjoy every moment of your exile to the country."

"What exile?" she inquired, but they had entered the manor, and Adrian had no further time to comment.

The housekeeper had assembled the staff in the entrance, and they began to offer their congratulations before Adrian and Celia took their places in the dining room. Conversations began to swirl around Celia, but her mind continued to attempt to understand Adrian's words regarding her exile. Surely he did not mean to leave her at his country estate, did he?

With their wedding reception over, Adrian asked for his coach to be brought around. There would be no dancing, nor had any been planned. Her trunks had already been packed and taken to his manor in Saltford, and there was no reason to delay their departure.

Her mother and sisters were teary eyed as they said their goodbyes. Her father gave her cheek a short kiss, but Celia knew it was only for show since others were present and such a moment of affection would be expected.

Their carriage ride was short, and before long, Celia

was being ushered inside Adrian's country home and up to her bedchamber. Celia took a moment to appreciate the pink floral wallpaper along with the comfortable-looking bed and its pink striped comforter. Two sitting chairs with a table between them sat before a fireplace. She saw that her things had already been unpacked, including her hairbrush and perfume vials, which were placed on a vanity for her use. If she had not known better, she would have said Adrian had had the room decorated just for her, pink being her favorite color.

Adrian stood in the doorway and peered inside. "I hope the room will meet your needs," he said, before leaning against the frame.

"I am certain the room will be fine, my lord," Celia replied, watching him carefully. "It is lovely. Thank you."

He came inside and went to the window to pull back the drapery before letting it fall back into place when his attention came back to rest upon her. "I will have a maid assigned to assist you as needed."

"I would appreciate such a kindness," she said, still observing him in the hope that he might soften his feelings towards her. "Will you be joining—"

A laugh burst from his lips. "Joining you? Hardly, my dear."

"But..." Celia's face flamed with heat, unsure how she dare ask if he would not consummate their marriage. She looked at a door to her right. "Is your room... near?"

Adrian went to the door and opened it. "This is a

bathing room for your use. My bedroom is in the east wing where you are not allowed to enter while I am in residence here."

"But what about..." her voice trailed off, embarrassed at the thought of remaining a virgin on her wedding night.

"You may keep your virginity, madam, and all the trappings that go with it. You have my name and now your reputation will be above reproach... at least after the gossip dies down. By the next season, something else will keep the *ton* amused, not that you shall be around to add to anything going on about town."

"You cannot keep me hidden away as though I do not exist, Adrian," she fumed.

He laughed again, causing Celia to flinch at the cruel sound. "Oh, but I can, my dear. You are my wife, to do with as I please, and at this particular moment, my only desire is to leave you here to contemplate your actions. Now, if you will excuse me, I plan to have a well-deserved drink before I retire for the evening... alone."

"Adrian, can we not discuss this?"

"No. As a matter of fact, I shall be leaving bright and early in the morning to return to London. Enjoy the country life, wife."

Without a backward glance, he left, slamming the door behind him. Celia's legs buckled beneath her. Falling to the floor, she wept, knowing her life would never be the same.

CHAPTER 14

January, 1815

Celia looked up from the letter she had been writing to her mother. She heard the unmistakable sounds of an arriving carriage followed by a wave of raised voices. Going to the window, she saw the familiar faces of her sisters in the courtyard, but also Uncle Nicolas, Grace, and Miranda, of all people.

She pulled the bell cord so her maid could help her dress. By the time she descended the stairway, her family was happily seated in the front parlor. A trolley sat near Elinor who was pouring tea and handing a cup to Alice.

"What a pleasant surprise," Celia announced as she entered the room. Her eyes fell on Miranda who quickly placed her cup on the table in front of her and stood.

"I came with reinforcements," Miranda began,

wringing her hands.

Celia looked around the room feeling a bitter sense of betrayal. She had repeatedly told those she loved she had no desire to speak with Miranda. "I see..."

"I am humbly asking you to forgive me, Celia. It was a horrible thing to do to you... and Adrian, of course."

"Yes... it was," Celia said, moving across the room with Miranda following close behind. She went to sit on the cushions of a rounded window seat to look out over the gardens that would bloom again once winter turned to spring. "How could you do something so horrible to me, Miranda? We were not merely friends but family. Family should not be so cruel to one another."

Miranda took Celia's hands. "I know, and for my vicious lies, I am most sorry," her voice shook and tears began to fall down her cheeks. "I was blinded by not having a titled husband of my own, and Phillip seemed the logical choice, especially since you did not want him."

Celia shivered, remembering her own ordeal with the man who tried to take her in the garden maze months ago. "Trust me, Miranda, you do not want him either. He is no gentleman."

"I also knew you and my brother cared for one another. I thought perhaps pushing you together would bring about your union," Miranda said before her face flushed with embarrassment. "My motives may have been sincere, but everything went farther than I had expected, and for that, I am sorry."

"You may be sorry, but now I am trapped in a marriage to a man I love who will not give me the time of day. You have doomed us to never finding happiness, Miranda." A worried frown marred her features. "How am I to earn Adrian's trust if he will not even be in the same house I am in, let alone the same room?"

Her uncle came to stand next to her, his hand resting upon her shoulder. "We have a plan to aid you, dear niece," Nicolas replied with a grin of conspiracy. He took her hand, and they made their way back to the group.

Celia sat before looking around at her family. "I believe I have had enough of plans made by others."

Grace took a sip of her tea. "My brother is miserable in London, and the situation between the two of you is intolerable. We have come to fix that."

Celia gave a short laugh. "And exactly how are we going to go about fixing that? I take it he does not believe Miranda's apologies?"

"He will not see me," Miranda explained. "Every time Grace or Nicolas has tried to speak to him, he stands up and leaves the room. He told Grace that he burns my letters unopened."

Tears threatened, but Celia blinked them back. "Then it is hopeless."

Elinor leaned back in her seat. "There is to be a Valentine's Day Ball in the Upper Assembly Rooms in Bath next month. You should attend."

Celia's eyes widened. "Why?"

Miranda clapped her hands. "Because by that time, word will have reached Adrian that you have taken over the east wing of this manor. He shall be furious that you went against his instructions and waste no time in returning to set the matter right... at least in his eyes."

Celia frowned. "How do you know about—"

"Because we know our brother," Grace interjected. "He is stubborn to a fault, but I also know he cares for you. His pride is hurt. He only needs a little push in the right direction so you both might begin again."

Celia rolled her eyes. "Such an action might send him over the edge. I have been on the receiving end of his anger. I do not care to push the limits of whatever self-control he still clings to when it comes to our marriage."

Nicolas began to pace before the women. "Now is the time to be brave, my dearest niece. If you want your marriage to be everything you have ever hoped for, you must reconcile your differences, but first, you must get Adrian to the country instead of languishing away in London. He has had enough time to calm down and get over his sense of betrayal. Perhaps now he will listen, for at the moment, this is all simply pure stubbornness on his part."

As she listened to their plan, Celia began to believe this crazy idea of theirs might actually work. Adrian was going to be furious with her, but his hatred might be worth suffering through if in the end she had his love.

CHAPTER 15

February, 1815

Adrian sat in an overstuffed chair inside Josephine's parlor, a much-needed drink in his hand. Josephine leaned forward and placed a hand on his knee, then began to slide her way up his thigh. His body stiffened in response and not in a good way. *God, what am I doing here?*

He leapt out of the chair and gulped down his drink. "I must go."

He had made a terrible mistake in coming here. When he had ordered his driver to this address, his thought had been to punish Celia, in a round-about way, by wiling away the day in his ex-mistress's arms. Now, he knew he could in no way betray the vows he had made to his wife nine weeks ago, despite the fact he had not seen her since.

Josephine stood and offered her hand. "Come upstairs, my lord. Let me make you forget..." her words trailed off, and her eyes sparkled with interest.

He gave her a brief smile. "If only it were that simple. This was a mistake."

She gave a light laugh. "You cannot blame me for trying, Adrian." She took his jacket from the back of a chair and helped him don the garment.

He took her hand and bowed over it. "Good-bye, Josephine."

She reached out to clasp the edges of his coat before placing a kiss on his cheek. "Farewell, Adrian. Please do not return unless you will stay. I do not think my heart could take another one of your departures."

He walked with her into the foyer and took his hat from her butler. "Understood."

Adrian left without looking back, not wishing to see Josephine's tearful face in the window again, and ordered his driver to return to his town house. He had been unfair to her by coming here. Perhaps, Josephine was not the only one he had been unfair to?

Adrian had resigned himself to his and Celia's current living arrangements. His pride still stung, and he could not get past it to begin mending the rift between them. He had refused Miranda's pleas, conveyed through Grace, to stay with him for the season. She and his wife could both stay in the country-side. As long as they remained there, he could not possibly be involved with any more of their shenanigans.

He had arrived home and had just poured himself a snifter of brandy in his study when he was interrupted.

"Lord Nicolas Lacey is here to see you, milord," his butler said.

"Show him in, Bradford," Adrian said, pouring another glass and handing it to his brother-in-law when he entered.

"Hello, Adrian. I thought I saw your carriage before it pulled around to the mews out back. Thought I might be mistaken, but here you are." Nicolas accepted the drink and took a chair near the fire.

"What brings you here?" Adrian asked.

"I might ask you what you are doing here instead of Bath for the ball in a couple of days with a fair part of Society in attendance," Nicolas replied before taking a sip of his brandy.

"There are plenty of balls to attend here in London if I so desire, which I do not," Adrian replied, dryly.

"Gracie will not speak to me for a week if I do not return there in time for the damn thing. It is to celebrate Valentine's Day, and she is set on attending.

Adrian cursed beneath his breath. A holiday for lovers, and one he wished never existed. "All the more reason for me to stay here in London. I have no desire to attend a ball made for happy couples."

Nicolas frowned. "But I thought you were attending with Celia. Grace said she would be there as well."

"Grace must have misunderstood. I gave specific instructions to Celia she was not to leave the manor."

"I am afraid I must be the bearer of bad news then, Adrian. I know for a fact Celia plans to attend. I was actually there when they were discussing their dresses, though I cannot say I cared to listen to all the details of lace and ribbons and such."

Heat rose to Adrian's face. "She would not dare go against my orders."

Nicolas shrugged. "I must have been mistaken then. I could have sworn my niece was positively beaming the last time I saw her. Made me believe you'd finally listened to Miranda, who has been trying to tell you for months that Celia knew nothing about her schemes, and was as shocked as you to have a sudden audience to her state. Which, I understand, was not in the least her fault! Why, I heard Celia has even moved into the east wing and is happily ensconced in your bedroom... not that I want to think of my niece in that way, but you *are* married to her."

"She has what?" Adrian slammed his glass down and watched the liquor slosh over the rim from the force.

Nicolas waved his glass in the air. "I understand from Grace that my niece plans a complete remodel of the interior, money being no object, or so Celia said. Apparently, Celia told my wife the manor appeared too manly and needed a woman's touch to make it more liveable."

"She would not dare," Adrian fumed.

"Oh, yes, she would. Good heavens man... did you not settle an allowance on the young woman? Those Lacey girls have quite expensive taste, if you did not know." Nicolas laughed. "My brother constantly complains they would land him in the poor house if he did not keep a tight hold on their spending."

Adrian stood, but not before gulping down the rest of his drink. "If you would excuse me, Nicolas. It appears a much needed discussion with my wife is long overdue."

"Of course. I must be getting back myself. Do not want to get on the bad side of my wife. Such does not make for an amicable marriage."

Adrian left his study but not before he heard Nicolas's laughter. He was unsure what the man thought was so funny. But Adrian had arrangements he must make before he could just pick up and leave for the country. He would be lucky to make it in time for the ball. Feeling wretched about how he treated Celia when he was trying to be angry about the refurbishment probably did not help.

⚜

Celia looked around the room, satisfied with the transformation of Adrian's bedroom. She had not changed much, only a few little touches here and there. Her vanity had been brought in from the other wing, as had a full-length mirror. Her dresses now hung next to the few remaining clothes Adrian had not taken with him when he left. She ran her fingers over one of his jackets, while she prayed to the heavens above that her husband would return her affections.

She went to sit at his writing desk. Taking up the quill, she dipped it in the ink before she began writing, a smile etching its way across her face while she thought of Adrian finding it on his pillow when he returned. Once finished, she sealed it with wax and placed it on his... their... bed, next to a boutonniere she had made for his jacket. Only when she saw him wearing the corsage would she know that all would be well between them.

Celia picked up her gloves and fan. She lingered with her hand on the door knob to look back at the rose petals brought in from the hothouse. They were scattered on the floor, leaving a pink trail to their bed. Even the bedcover had petals upon it.

She hoped he would view this in the manner she intended; to let the past rest where it should and begin their lives anew. A Valentine's Day wish from her heart to his. She closed the door with a smile. Fate would decide the next direction her life would follow.

CHAPTER 16

Adrian walked inside his country manor in Saltford and gazed around the foyer. Flowers sat in a vase on a table where he noticed a few invitations waited to be opened. A servant took his outer cloak and hat even while Adrian's attention went to the front parlor.

Normally, he might not have paid much attention to the subtle transformations done to the room. But it was hard not to notice the dark wooden panels on the walls had been stripped and replaced with a pleasant shade of cream-colored wallpaper that made the room welcoming. Adrian cleared his throat, and a bit of the anger he had been holding onto all the way from London melted away. If these were the changes Celia had been doing while he was gone, he would not chastise her for redecorating. She had a good eye for color schemes. Still, her leaving the manor without him continued to bother him.

"Welcome home, my lord," his housekeeper said. "Your valet has your clothes laid out as her ladyship directed. She knew you might be running late."

His brow rose at Celia's audacity. "Where is the Countess?" he asked while he began climbing the stairs to his bedroom.

"Her ladyship has gone ahead of you, sir, and told me to inform you she would see you at the ball in Bath."

In the east wing, he opened his bedroom door and stood in shock, his mouth dropping open. He had expected to see massive changes to the room. Only a few of the items he had purchased for Celia were now placed in the room. But it was the rose petals thrown upon the floor making their way up to the bed that caused the ice surrounding his heart to crack open.

He noticed a letter placed near his pillow, and he went to pick it up, along with a boutonniere lying next to it. He inhaled the floral scent of the pink rose nestled within some greenery. The smell reminded him of everything about his wife that he had come to love. He broke open the wax seal and read her letter.

My Dearest Adrian:

Please forget any thoughts of betrayal about me that may still linger in your mind. I had no part in your sister's plan and only wanted your love to call my own from the moment we met at Hollystone. I will never love another as I love you, my dearest husband. Please wear this rose tonight as a sign we can start over again and meet me in Bath for the Valentine's Day Ball. Will you be my Valentine, Adrian?

Your loving wife,
Celia

The last of his anger melted away, and with it, he opened his mind to the fact he had been unfair to Celia. He had been a fool to believe Celia would play such a trick. Miranda, yes, and he could even believe she would lie afterwards. If Nicolas was to be believed, she had tried to confess once she calmed down, but Adrian had refused to speak to her, refused even to read her letters. He did not deserve Celia, and he had been wrong to blame her all this time. She had every right to be angry. But the letter suggested she was willing to let the past settle and move forward with their lives. He began to change his clothes. It was never good to keep a lady waiting.

Celia followed a servant through the crowded tearoom in the Upper Assembly rooms. It was the same servant who had found her near the ballroom entrance, craning her neck to witness Adrian's arrival, but there had still been no sign of him. She was unsure who wished to urgently speak to her, but Celia supposed she could manage a few moments of her time. A reprieve in waiting for her husband's arrival might be just what she needed to calm her nerves.

The servant held out a chair for her, and Celia sat across from a woman with dark black hair. She was older than Celia by several years, but Celia could not miss the worry in the woman's eyes.

"My apologies for keeping you waiting, Mrs. Bouchard, but the crowd has become overly large, making it hard to move from room to room.

"You were very kind to meet with me, my lady," the woman said, her gaze scanning the room.

"You will have to forgive me, but I am not certain we have been introduced. Have we met before?" Celia inquired, trying to figure out where she might have met the lady.

"Good heavens, no. I am certain we do not run in the same circles. You are very beautiful... and so young. No wonder Adrian is infatuated." Mrs. Bouchard's tone was breathy, while her eyes continued her inspection of Celia.

Celia's eyes narrowed at Adrian's given name being murmured so informally from the lips of another woman. She tried to calm her racing heart at the implications of this impromptu meeting. "What can I do for you, Mrs. Bouchard?"

"I do not suppose you would consider leaving Adrian? Obviously, the two of you do not have a loving marriage, if the rumors I have heard are true." She opened her reticule and slid a bank draft across the table. "This should see you comfortably settled and see to your needs for years to come."

Celia stared at the note, the numbers becoming a blur in her mind as she began to realize who this woman might be. Celia leaned forward in order for their conversation to not be overheard. "Are you attempting to tell me that you and my husband are lovers?"

Mrs. Bouchard gave her a sheepish smile. "I would do anything in the world to keep him with me."

"And you feel that having this public meeting will see me gone, just because you wish it?" Celia hissed, even while she fought back tears.

The woman raised her eyes to meet Celia's. "I love him," she stated in a hushed tone.

"Then, we at least have that in common, Mrs. Bouchard, because I love him, too." Celia slipped the note back across the table. "You may keep your money."

"Very well," Mrs. Bouchard stated. Defeat washed across the woman's features as she tucked the note back inside her reticule, only to pull out a black leather glove. "Please give this to Adrian. He left it at my house the other day."

Celia stared at the glove as though it had bitten

away at a piece of her heart. Jealousy coursed through her at the thought of what Adrian had shared with the woman across the table. The glove was familiar to her, since she was the one who had given it to him at the first Christmas the Laceys and de Courtenays had shared as a family.

She took up the glove and stood. "Excuse me…" Celia said as she left the table. She could not stand to be in this woman's presence a minute longer.

All her plans were for naught! Adrian did not care for her nor would he ever, not when he had a beautiful mistress at hand to see to his needs. And to think they had been together just days before, while Celia was trying to prepare a reunion with her husband. She was such a fool… again!

☙❦❧

Adrian entered the ballroom and saw his wife across the room, looking particularly lovely in a pink-tinted gown. His brows narrowed in concern, however, as he observed her from the distance. She appeared as though something was bothering her. He looked around, seeing his sisters along with Celia's. Wyndham was also present, but he was luckily nowhere near Miranda, for once, and he was grateful the man adhered to his order to stay clear of his sister. So what was bothering his wife? He thought that this dance would be a happy occasion.

And then he saw the reason. Josephine. What the devil was she doing here? She waved to him at the entrance to the ballroom and had the nerve to blow him a kiss. He immediately turned from her sight to see the stricken look wash across his wife's face as she witnessed Josephine's sign of affection.

Adrian gave Josephine no further thought. His only wish was to reach his wife. He came up behind her, and the familiar scent of her perfume spiraled up to assault his senses. This had always been the case with his little sparrow. God only knew how much he had yearned for her, especially knowing she was legally now his wife.

"I have missed you," he confessed, whispering in her ear. He did not miss her shiver, and he was glad to know he had the same effect on her.

"Have you?" Celia murmured. He attempted to gently turn her around, but she continued to keep her back towards him.

"Yes, I have," he crooned lovingly while bringing her closer into his embrace. "The note you left behind for me gave me hope for our future life together as husband and wife."

"I should never have written that letter. As you once said, love and marriage do not belong together. Such a belief is just a myth."

Did she mean to make him suffer for doubting her? He supposed he deserved it. "What? No. I was wrong when I said that. Plus, you, my darling Celia, do not truly believe that. I am so sorry for not believing you. I will make it up to you, I promise. Can you not forgive me?"

She fumbled with something before she handed a glove to him over her shoulder while she continued to refuse to turn around so they could speak eye to eye. He took the glove, wondering where he had misplaced it.

"Your mistress asked that I return this to you since you conveniently left it at her home the other day. Perhaps, if you hurry, you can still meet her." Celia waved her hand towards the crowd. "She is here somewhere."

A sob escaped Celia before she wrenched herself from his arms to make her way across the room. Adrian silently stood there fuming. *Damn Josephine to hell!* Just when he thought he and Celia were on their way to finding a common accord, his ex-mistress had to muddle things up. No... *he* muddled things up by going back there in the first place. And he had to put them right.

He came up behind his wife, whose shoulders shook as tears streaked down her face. He placed his hands upon her shoulders. "I am sorry she upset you, Celia," he apologized. "It was wrong for me to go to her, and I did not stay long. I knew I had made a mistake the moment I entered her house. I left almost as soon as I had arrived."

"You did?" Celia asked, her hushed tone hopeful.

"Yes, I did. And darling, nothing happened." Relief flooded through Adrian when Celia leaned back into his chest. He wrapped his arms around her, and he cared not if the entire *ton* saw their display of affection.

"She told me she loved you."

Adrian shook his head. "She must be very desperate to try to hold onto something she never had in the first place, my dear, because she knows how very much I love my wife."

"Y–you l–love me?"

"Yes. I do. I love you. Besides, how could I not love a woman who asked me to be her Valentine?"

A gasp escaped Celia, and she quickly turned in his arms. Her eyes widened, and she fingered the corsage on the lapel of his jacket. "You wore it..." her voice faded away as fresh tears fell from her eyes.

He pulled a chain from inside his coat and held up his birthday gift to her, the little bird sparkling in the candlelight of the room. He had had the broken clasp repaired months ago, and it gave him great pleasure to once again fasten the necklace around Celia's neck. "Promise me you shall never take this off again, unless I am replacing it with some other bauble that is worthy of my Countess."

Celia clapped her hand over her mouth to hide her surprise. "You found it! I thought it was lost forever."

"Promise me," he urged, while leaning down to place his forehead on hers. He waited for her response as if this was a vow to one another for a new beginning.

"Yes, I promise, Adrian," she cried out.

Relief swept over him at her declaration. "Tell me

those are tears of happiness," Adrian demanded, while he brushed the wetness from his wife's cheeks.

Celia nodded while a beautiful smile curved her lips. "Tell me again you love me, Adrian, so I can remember this moment for the rest of our lives together," she said in a breathy whisper.

He gave her a roguish grin before bending down to place a kiss upon her lips. "I love you, my dearest wife. Tell me... will you be mine for today and all of our tomorrows?"

Celia reached up to caress his cheek. She never appeared lovelier than she did at this exact moment. "I love you, Adrian; until the end of all eternity, I will love only you.

He kissed her lips once more, even while the chords of a waltz began to play. "I believe they are playing our song, my love."

"We have a song?"

"We do now. Shall we?" he extended his arm and swung his wife into the dance.

As Adrian began twirling his lady around the ball-room, his heart filled with joy. From this day forward, the past was behind them, and their future seemed bright. With Celia in his arms, he would look forward to their years together as husband and wife.

EPILOGUE

Saltford
One Year Later

Celia looked down at her sleeping son. The baby
briefly opened his eyes before yawning and going
back to sleep. She kissed his downy head before looking
up into the eyes of her husband, who was tying the sash
to his robe as he entered the room.

"Has he finally drifted off?" he quietly asked, leaning
over to take the sleeping bundle from her arms.

"Yes, and if we are lucky, he may sleep for the next
several hours," Celia softly whispered. She watched
Adrian hand the child to the nanny who stood just
outside their bedroom door.

He returned to her side with a sly grin. "I wonder
what we could do with so much time to ourselves."

Sitting up in the bed, Celia laughed before pulling back the covers of the bed for him to join her. "Sleep?" she teased.

Adrian laughed. "I am certain we can come up with something a little more... stimulating," he said before nibbling at her neck.

Her breath left her when her husband started the fire within her that burned only for him. She undid the sash to let the robe fall from his body. Her hungry eyes roamed over every inch of him, and she held out her hand for him to join her.

Adrian groaned. "I shall never tire of seeing you with such a look in your eyes, my love." He reached over to the side dresser, lifting a lid on a ceramic bowl before placing it down on the table. Her husband's smile was truly wicked before he lifted the bowl to tilt the contents over her body. Soft pink rose petals tickled her as they fell upon her and also landed on the sheets.

"I am glad to see you still remember my Valentine's Day offering, my darling husband."

Adrian joined her in their bed. "How could I ever forget? We shall celebrate our love for years to come, and I will always shower you with roses whenever I am able. I love you, Celia."

She pulled him down next to her. "Show me..."

And he did... for that night and for many years to come. Her earl may have been reluctant to take her to wife, but there were no further barriers hindering their happiness. Their lives were complete, and Celia could not ask Adrian to love her more than he showed her each and every night. They had found love. She was content.

Medieval & Time Travel Series

To Love A Scottish Laird: De Wolfe Pack Connected World

Sometimes you really can fall in love at first sight...

Lady Catherine de Wolfe knows she must find a husband before her brother chooses one for her. A tournament to celebrate the wedding of the Duke of Normandy might be her answer. She does not expect to fall for a man after just one touch. Laird Douglas MacLaren of Berwyck is invited to the tournament by the Duke of Normandy. He goes to ensure Berwyck's safety once Henry takes the throne. He does not expect to become entranced by a woman who bumps into him. Yet, nothing is ever quite that simple. Not everyone is happy with the union of this English lady and a Scottish laird. From the shores of France, to Berwyck Castle on the border between their countries, Douglas and Catherine must find their way to protect their newfound love.

If My Heart Could See You: The MacLaren's, Book One

When you're enemies, does love have a fighting chance? Amiria of Berwyck vows to protect her people by pledging her oath of fealty to the very enemy who has laid siege to her home. Dristan, the Devil's Dragon of Blackmore, has a reputation to uphold as champion knight of his king. Lies, treachery, and deceit attempt to tear them apart, but only love will bring them together

For All of Ever: The Knights of Berwyck, A Quest Through Time (Book One)

Sometimes to find your future, you must look to the past... Katherine dreamed of her knight all her life yet how could she know she'd be thrown back into the past? Nothing prepares Riorden for the beautiful vision of a strangely clad ghost appearing in his chamber. Centuries keep them apart but will Time give them a chance at finding love?

Only For You: The Knights of Berwyck, A Quest Through Time (Book Two)

Sometimes it's hard to remember that true love conquers all, only after the battle is over... Katherine has it all but settling into her duties at Warkworth is dangerous to her well-being. Consumed with memories of his father, Riorden must deal with his sire's widow. Torn apart, Time becomes their enemy while Marguerite continues her ploy to keep Riorden at her side. With all hope lost, will Katherine & Riorden find a way to save their marriage?

Hearts Across Time: The Knights of Berwyck (Books One & Two)

Sometimes all you need is to just believe... Hearts Across Time is a special edition box set that combines Katherine and Riorden's stories together from *For All of Ever* and *Only For You.*

A Knight To Call My Own: The MacLaren's, Book Two

When your heart is broken, is love still worth the risk? Lynet of Clan MacLaren knows how it feels to love someone and not have that love returned. Ian MacGillivray has returned to Berwyck in search of a bride. Who will claim the fair Lynet? The price will be high to ensure her safety and even higher to win her love.

To Follow My Heart: The Knights of Berwyck, A Quest Through Time (Book Three)

Love is a leap. Sometimes you need to jump... Jenna Sinclair is dealing with a horrendous break up with her fiancé when she finds herself pulled through time to twelfth century England. Fletcher Monroe has spent too much time pining away for a woman who will never be his until a strangely clad woman magically appears. Torn between the past and the present, will their growing love survive a journey through Time?

The Piper's Lady in Never Too Late, A Bluestocking Belles Collection 2017

True love binds them. Deceit divides them. Will they choose love?

Lady Coira Easton spent her youth traveling with her grandfather. Now well past the age men prefer when they choose a wife, she has resigned herself to remain a maiden. But everything changes once she arrives at Berwyck Castle. She cannot resist a dashing knight who runs to her rescue, but would he give her a second look?

Garrick of Clan MacLaren can hold his own with the trained Knights of Berwyck, but as the clan's piper they would rather he play his instruments to entertain them—or lead them into battle—than to fight with a sword upon the lists. Only when he sees a lady across the training field and his heart sings for the first time does he begin to wish to be something he is not.

Will a simple misunderstanding between them threaten what they have found in one another or will they at last let love into their hearts?

One Last Kiss: The Knights of Berwyck, A Quest Through Time, Book 5

Sometimes it takes a miracle to find your heart's desire...

Scotland, 1182: Banished from his homeland, Thomas of Clan Kincaid lives among distant relatives, reluctantly accepting he may never return home... until the castle's healer tells him of a woman traveling across time...

Dare he believe the impossible?

Present Day, Michigan: Jade Calloway is used to being alone, and as Christmas approaches, she's skeptical when told she'll embark on an extraordinary journey. But when a ring magically appears, and she sees a ghostly man in her dreams...

Dare she believe in the possible?

Regency's

A Kiss For Charity: A de Courtenay Novella (Book One)

Love heals all wounds but will their pride keep them apart?

Young widow, Grace, Lady de Courtenay, has no idea how a close encounter with a rake at a masquerade ball would make her yearn for love again. Lord Nicholas Lacey is captivated by a lovely young woman he encounters at a masquerade. Considering the company she keeps, she might be interested in becoming his mistress. From the darkened paths of Vauxhall Gardens to a countryside estate called Hollystone Hall, Nicholas and Grace must set aside their differences in order to let love into their hearts.

The Earl Takes A Wife: A de Courtenay Novella (Book Two)

It began with a memory, etched in the heart.

Lady Celia Lacey is too young for a husband, especially man-about-town Lord Adrian de Courtenay. But when she meets him at a house party, she falls in love.

Adrian finds the appealing innocent impossible to forget, though she is barely out of the schoolroom and a relative by marriage.

His sister's deception brings them together, but destroys their happiness. Can they reach past the hurt to the love that still burns?

Nothing But Time: A Family of Worth, Book One

They will risk everything for their forbidden love...

When Lady Gwendolyn Marie Worthington is forced to marry a man old enough to be her father, she concludes love will never enter her life. Her husband is a cruel man who blames her for his own failings. Then she meets her brother's attractive business associate, and all those longings she had thought gone forever suddenly reappear.

A long-term romance holds no appeal for Neville Quinn, Earl

of Drayton until an unexpected encounter with the sister of the Duke of Hartford. Still, he resists giving his heart to another woman, especially one who belongs to another man.

Chance encounters lead to intimate dinners, until Neville and Gwendolyn flee to Berwyck Castle at Scotland's border hoping beyond reason their fragile love will survive the vindictive reach of Gwendolyn's possessive husband. Before their journey is over, Gwendolyn will risk losing the only love she has ever known.

One Moment In Time: A Family of Worth, Book Two

One moment in time may be enough, if it lasts forever...

When the man Lady Roselyn Anne Winslow has loved since she was a young girl begins to court her, Roselyn thinks all her dreams have come true... until the dream turns into a nightmare.

Lady Roselyn is everything Edmond Worthington, 9th Duke of Hartford, could ask for in a wife and he is delighted to find she returns his love... until he loses her, not once but twice.

From England's ballrooms, to Berwyck Castle and a tropical island that is anything but paradise, Edmond and Roselyn face ruthless enemies who will do anything to tear them apart. Can they recover their one moment in time?

Under the Mistletoe

A new suitor seeks her hand. An old flame holds her heart. Which one will she meet under the kissing bough? When Margaret Templeton is requested to act as hostess at a Christmas party she did not think she would see the man who once held her heart. Frederick Maddock, Viscount Beacham never forgot the young woman he had fallen in love with. Will the two finally put down their differences and once again fall in love?

You can find out more about Sherry's work on her website at www.SherryEwing.com and at online retailers.

SOCIAL MEDIA

Website: www.SherryEwing.com
Email: Sherry@SherryEwing.com
Bluestocking Belles: www.bluestockingbelles.net/
Amazon Author Page: http://amzn.to/1TrWtoy
Bookbub: www.bookbub.com/authors/sherry-ewing
Facebook: www.Facebook.com/SherryEwingAuthor
Goodreads: www.Goodreads.com/author/show/
8382315.Sherry_Ewing
Instagram: https://instagram.com/sherry.ewing
Pinterest: www.Pinterest.com/SherryLEwing
Tumblr: https://sherryewing.tumblr.com
Twitter: www.Twitter.com/Sherry_Ewing
YouTube: http://www.youtube.com/SherryEwingauthor

Sign Me Up!
Newsletter: http://bit.ly/2vGrqQM
Facebook Street Team:
www.facebook.com/groups/799623313455472/
Facebook Official Fan page: https://www.facebook.com/
groups/356905935241836/

COMING SOON

To Love An English Knight:
De Wolfe Pack Connected World

and

Love Will Find You:
The Knights of Berwyck A Quest Through Time
(Book Four)

ABOUT SHERRY EWING

Sherry Ewing picked up her first historical romance when she was a teenager and has been hooked ever since. A bestselling author, she writes historical and time travel romances to awaken the soul one heart at a time. When not writing, she can be found in the San Francisco area at her day job as an Information Technology Specialist.

Learn more about Sherry at:
Website: www.SherryEwing.com
Email: Sherry@SherryEwing.com

Printed in Great Britain
by Amazon

69613595R00095